Alphonse Yochum

Perplexities: An American comedy-drama

In four acts and six tableaux

Alphonse Yochum

Perplexities: An American comedy-drama
In four acts and six tableaux

ISBN/EAN: 9783337224493

Printed in Europe, USA, Canada, Australia, Japan

Cover: Foto ©Andreas Hilbeck / pixelio.de

More available books at **www.hansebooks.com**

PERPLEXITIES,

An American Comedy—Drama,

IN

FOUR ACTS and SIX TABLEAUX.

BY

ALPHONSE M. YOCHUM,

PRINTED—NOT PUBLISHED.

PERPLEXITIES.

————:o:————

ACT I. TABLEAU I.

Exterior of the Female College and Grounds in Indianapolis.—Col lege, with steps, door, call bell &c. R.—The Little Globe Hotel, with sign &c., in the distance at back L—Rustic chairs vasese, &c., L and at back.

Enter Jayen Faul, with violin.

Jayen.   He is here ! I have seen him ! The monster has safely arrived !   Now can I despair, or, secure a cell at Dr. Phaeton's Asylum.   Aurora is lost to me forever; Aurora, with that sweet, that beautiful name, Elena Mayflower.   In eight days she will be Madam Hartfield—Oh, I shall go mad—mad ! She loves me, but it is no heroic love ; she will not die, no, no, not even elope with me ! Oh, curses on that Ignatius Mohr, the paragon of the most cunning. Why did you desert your old friend ? Did I not write you the most movable letters, and still more, did I not advance your tracling expenses ? Since fourteen days past you could have been here— here, within the bounds of fame for your precious talent, but you did not come, barbarian and my last hopes vanish,

Enter Ignatius Mohr.

Mohr.   A great city indeed.   Every other house—a restaurant or a winehouse, or a coffee stand.   The sidewalks are crowded with putrid fellows, whose philosophy is naught else but to blockade the pathway of the industrious, and thus idly gaze at earths daily toils —Here is another of the same stripe, perchance, he can direct me to Jayen Faul.—Excuse me sir. where—'tis Jayen himself, give me your hand ! (goes to shake hands with Jayen, who does not recognize him.)

Jayen   Who are you ?

Mohr.   Know me, Jayen?   Ignatius Mohr !

Jayen   Mohr ! You have changed considerably since last I've seen you—strange, you have quite a large beard now, I did not recognize you.

Mohr. Oh yea, the world you know is full of changes and as the tide of time rolls on, so do we move on in years.

Jayen. So you have come at last!

Mohr. With heart and soul at your service.

Jayen. Tis scarce a minute since I wished you to all the devils.

Mohr. Be cautious of what you say. I have brought all the devils with me.

Jayen. Where have you been, why did you not come sooner?

Mohr. Ha, from Chicago to Indianapolis is not a *cat's* leap.

Jayen. But remember, a railway coach is *not* a cat.

Mohr. Not much better, I have traveled all this distance afoot.

Jayen. What, did I not send you money, and that in abundance too?

Mohr. But my debts were still *more* abundant. I could not quit the city till I had paid all. In vain I offered to pawn my young wife.

Jayen. How, you are married?

Mohr. Certainly. She has come with me, I have taught her to —(aside.) what would I say, I must not betray myself—a—a she is nimble and sly, and perhaps we can make her useful.

Jayen. And she too did walk this great distance?

Mohr. Well that's a question! It wouldn't do for me to tell you, that, like some evil genius she hovered around me.

Jayen. How did you gain a subsistence?

Mohr. In the most profitable manner certainly (aside.) that you shall soon learn.

Jayen. Alas, Ignatius! you have come to late!

Mohr. Who has come too late? Never say *too late*. We shall see, speak, why did you summon me here, what would you have me do?

Jayen. I am in love.

Mohr. Again! I was just going to tell you, that some of your former affections whom you deserted, are still despairing.

Jayen. I am in love for the first time—

Mohr. You tell me that for the seventh time —

Jayen. With an angel whom I wished to make my wife.

Mohr. And what prevents you from doing so?

Jayen. See there (points to house it.) lives Madam De Ruyter, the proprietress of the Female Educational Institution, and with her scholars is the object of my passion.

Mohr. Doubtless yet a child?

Jayen. Childlike, but no more a child, an orphan possessing great wealth—

Mohr. (quickly) Real estate, or—

Jayen. And for whom I have a tender love and affection.

Mohr. That is secondary. Speak of the chief question; her name?

Jayen. Aurora Elena Mayflower! Her dying mother betrothe her to some awkward, silly, German farmer, in short, the bridegroom arrived to-day, and to morrow they leave for Delphi where they will be married.

Mohr. His name?

Jayen. Max Hartfelt!

Mohr. Wheugh! a spicy one.

Jayen. Listen to me: he is a native of Germany. About three years ago his father died, leaving him, the only heir, a large estate. which he subsequently disposed of and came to this country. Here he migrated to the West, and settled down in the suburbs of Delphi, about sixty miles from this place. There, he invested in a large farm, the earnings of which, in conjunction with the surplus of his inheritance. makes him the happy possessor of considerable wealth.

Mohr. Indeed!—What are his haunts, his peculiarities?

Jayen. He has a remarkably gourdy appearance; the tape indicates about six feet in circumference.

Mohr. Enough. I know my man. And you fear such a codfish?

Jayen. As if the richest codfish do not sometimes, or generally. snap up the most amiable women

Mohr. I think I understand the whole *status causae*: Your beloved is an Andromeda, thaeatened by some monster to be covered and devoured; *you*, are the Perseus striving to free her and *I* shall have the honor to represent your Pegasus.

Jayen. Right, right, but you come at the very moment in which the monster opens widely its jaws.

Mohr. The more honor will the victory bring.

Jayen. Do you think so?

Mohr. Love and cunningness in league: what power can resist?

Jayen. Should you succeed, I would clasp you to my heart.

Mohr. Nothing more?

Jayen. And your beautiful wife too.

Mohr. A great honor!

Jayen. And a grateful love will remember you till death.

Mohr. But, if that love dies first?

Jayen. That you need not fear.

Mohr. Not! Yet such an occurrence would not be singular. A good round sum would be preferable.

Jayen. Well, say fifty dollars.

Mohr. (contemptuously) Fifty dollars!

Jayen. Hundred dollars! — (Ignatius turns and says nothing Two hundred dollars—(aside) that's my whole fortune,—what say you? (no reply,—Jayen aside) Five hundred would be a cheap purchase, tho girl is rich. she is worth more than ten times that amount,—Five hundred dollars—

Mohr. (turns suddenly) That's a bargain, that's a premium. Ere twenty-four hours that pumpkin shall be far away from this place.

Jayen. Egad, that would be a masterstroke.

Mohr. But hold—to conduct a campaign, a good General must be acquainted with the country. So here lives Madam DeRuyter, and there is a restaurant—

Jayen. The "Little Globe" hotel, and there (points off I.) Doctor Phaeton's asylum, famous for the cure of lunatics.

Mohr. O-oh! doubtless he is well patronized?

Jayen. (Playfully) Yes, if fools would desire to be cured.

Mohr. I will remember him. And what large building is that with the tower?

Jayen. That is the City Hall and also the headquarters of the police.

Mohr. That will do for the present. But now I must have some—(gesticulating meaning money.)

Jayen. Why, and what for?

Mohr. Secret expenditures certainly, for without money, Satan himself would be a poor devil.

Jayen. There (gives money) there's fifty dollars.

Mohr. Now where can I find this hollow pretender?

Jayen. He is at the Depot Hotel and will soon appear at this heaven's gate.

Mohr Good. I shall be prepared for his reception. But, what would you with this violin, are you a dancing master?

Jayen. Just so Ignatius, for the reason of which I gain admission to Aurora's private apartment.

Mohr. You will be my accomplice, you will play whatever part I may assign to you?

Jayen. (With emphasy) Yes, I *will* play a part, but, listen to me: don't be serious, remember — I only want you to discourage him, nauseate him of the city so that he will be glad to get out of it again. Mark well my words, do him no harm, no bodily or moral injuries—*or I may play another part!*

Mohr. For the present you can play the dancing master and leave me, alone with **my** genius.

Jayen. Remember what I have told you Ignatius—

Mohr. Stop—do not call me Ignatius.

Jayen. And why not pray?

Mohr. Oh, merely to keep my name and the business you confided to me, a secret, anything but Ignatius—Edmund will do.

Jayen. For the present, farewell! Remember now, *mum* is the word, for neither Aurora nor her lover Max, shall know one word about this. (Has rang the door-bell.) Adieu! and may Cupid in all his wit reveal himself to you (Door is opened by servant, exit Jayen in door.)

Mohr Now I am again in my vocation. What else could I do! All the maidens virtuous, all women faithful—I could pilfer and deceive no longer; became to well known at the end, and unceasingly haunted after the death of my victim, was compelled to eave Chicago. I disappeared suddenly one night, and walked

from there to this place, thereby making it quite difficult to trace
me. Here, I have assumed another name, besides, this artifictal
beard conceals the scar in my face, which would otherwise betray
me; and with this new face I defy detection. There is now another
path spread before me, and—see, there's a huge object rolling this
way—everybody seems astonished—he answers Jayen's description
—as I live tis he, Max Hartfeld, nearing on the wings of love!
Max. (Without) Never mind, I fix em!

Enter Max, exhausted, hat in hand, wipes prespiration from his
brow and fans himself.

Max. I wonder where I vas now? (sighs with the exclamation)
Oh my! Dis town Indianapolis is so big dat I beleive I loose de
shtreet mit mineself
Caracelli. (Has entered) Can I do anyting a for-a you? (Taps
Max on shoulder, who turns quickly.)
Max. (Surveys him(Ye-e-s!
Caracelli. What?—
Max. Mind your own bustness!
Caracelli. Fine-a statue, Cicero—
Max. I don kno him—gone away, I don't want some.

(Exit Caracelli crying,) Statoots-a-La Napoleone.

Max. All hollow heads, dey don kno somedings.—Ef I only
find me dat shtreet, Aurora she—
Mohr, (Taps him on shoulder) Can I
' Max. (Turns quickly, striking Ignatius) Oh, I begs your bar-
don!
Mohr. Certainly, certainly—
Max. I dot you vas dat feller what sell dem paby dolls!
Mohr. Oh, that's alright! You are a stranger here I presume?
Max. Yes I vas, I ust comes mit de Union Railroad Depot! I
vas Max Hartfield von Delphi. I have some wool wat I sell, un
den I gone married.
Mohr. Indeed!—Wool of sheep?
Max. Ye-e-s, shoor, in Delphi you kno, de sheeps don't carry
cotton.
Mohr. No, certainly not. Have you chosen the bride?
Max. Aurora Mayflower, mit fourty dousand dollars. I bin
rich mineself, awer I don't got enough yet.
Mohr. Fathomless wisdom lies in these words.
Max. Is dat so? Well I like dat, dat wisdom comes to me
from mineself you kno.
Mohr. Do you love her?
Max. I love her! I love her alltimes, un she is so sweet, so
peautiful, so fair like milk un roses. She vas in Delphi onced, in
de harvest time, awer I don't see her. I take mine bride mit me
ter-morrow in Delphi, un den we gone married.
Mohr. Is she pretty?

Max, Ah, she vas a nice gerl, no dollpaby; for whatever I catch hold on, you see dem dogs? (shows fists.)

Mohr. I see!

Max. Wen I gone down shtreet I meet a womans wat have one basket full eggs, I only shake mine hand one little bit—bloomps—un dat basket lay in de mud. I must bay dem eggs!

Mohr. That was irksome.

Max. I don kno! After wile I meet somebody else wat have un umbreller, he bump on mine head un break dree ribs, he want me to bay dat umbreller, ye-e-s!

Mohr. Ah, that was hard.

Max. Dat feller he say mine *head* was so hard, in de hole town dere vas none so much like dat.

Mohr. Certainly. he was right, in fact it's a rarity, in perfect harmony with the entire body; tis a lovely aspect, your bride will be perfectly enraptured.

Max. En-wat?—I don kno wat dat was. She is in a shool of education mit a France womans, you kno were dat is?

Mohr, Perhaps you mean Madam DeRuyter!

Max. Ye-e-s, Madame DeRuyter. I kno dat outside.

Mohr. That is right here. Do you see that house?

Maq. Ye-e-s, dut's it!—Well now, I bin so near uf dat was a shnake he bite me. (laughs, crosses R) I'm so tired!

Mohr. In a strange place one often requires such information; if you desire a hired servant, I am at your command.

Max. A hired servant?—Dat is so much as one servant wat got baid?

Mohr. Generally speaking, yes, bu I'll serve *par honeur.*

Max. Par how many, is dat much?

Mohr. Sometimes very little.

Max. Well, if it vas wery little—

Mohr. I'll not demand one cent, merely the *honor* to serve such gallantry as yours.

Max. Is dat so? Well you shall have dat honor, wy not! Also you are mine servant?

Mohr. Exactly, yes!

Max. Who vas your name?

Mohr. (Aside(Let me see, what is my name- Dawvil—Speth Dawvil!

Max. Shpitten Devil, goot!

Mohr. No, no, *Speth Dawvil!*

Max. Oh I wont forgot em.

Mohr. I am known by everybody in Indianapolis, as an honest and upright man.

Max. Well mine honest Shpitten Devil, I'll give you some business right away, I got no time mineself,—You see dat baper I got dat baper in Delphi von de Shustice of de pease. He toll : . I gif dat hapers to de bolice office in Indianapolis. I don kno where dat is. I- I—don kno nottings.

Mohr. Give it to me, I will provide for it. [Max gives enve-lope containing letter of recomendation and credit.]

Max. Do dat mine dear Shpitten Devil. [Advances to house]

Mohr. Probably you will partake of a good meal with your bride?

Max. Ye-e s, I bin fond of meals, awer de beoples say, in de boarding shool dey don't got much, un ye kno I like many.

Mohr Then you may eat two meals.

Max. [Delighted] Two times! Will dot pass?

Mohr. Certainly, and then I will show you the sights of the city.

Max. Alright, I gone eaten two times, un you gif dat baper to de bolice office, den you comes quick right away back, I got son.e unner business vor you wen I gone married. [Catches hold of door knob and pushes.]

Mohr. [Aside] That you shall never be. [Aloud to Max] Ring the bell!

Max. Yes I will do dat! [pulls door knob]

Mohr No, no, the call bell to your right. [Max catches hold of bell knob] There, now pull.

Max. Well now, I forgot all about it. [pulls violently, breaks wire, bell is heard to ring, Max almost falls backward down steps.]

Mohr. You have pulled a little too hard!

Max. Well you kno, dat's my fashion. How I gone in?

Mohr. The servant will come to the door. [Servant opens door'

Max. Don't forgot wat I toll you! [exit in College]

Mohr. Ha, ha, ha! That's a prime plant, un ignoramus, a spec-imen of awkwardness. [Takes letter from envelope, reads it.] A letter of credit and recomendation to Max Hartfeld from a Delphi Notary Public, and this, [finds a bank check on tinted paper, reads:] Bank of Delphi, Indiana, June 21st, pay to bearer, Miss Aurora Elena Mayflower, the sum of five thousand dollars on ac-count, within one week from date, signed Max Hartfelt.—Ha, ha, ha! Precious! This will prove a little bonanza, sent to me by the devil, no doubt, if I but take advantage of the opportunity. To work then at once—but my promise to Jayen Faul—oh fie!—I'll try it, I will succeed, I *feel* I will succeed, for whenever I under-take anathing Ignatius Mohr never fails. Now to settle a plan of the campaign.—His departure to-morrow must be *prevented*—let me see--the letter of recommendation—the bank check—my wife I have it. I'll straight forward to the police headquarters, and —[nearing entrance] tis one of the highly honored officers that comes this way, with a pair of eyes resembling interrogation points. I'll try to win him, for, whoever passes through a strange village, *sans comparaison*, should take precaution and befriend the dogs. [retires—enter Bells Gap the officer, crosses—Mohr takes a $1 note from his vest pocket·] Pst, pst! sir!

Officer. What would you with me?

Mohr. Pardon my importunity—your an officer!

Officer. Yes sir, and am responsible for the peace and quietness of the beat in which you are.

Mohr. I am a stranger here, and find myself in a little perplexity.

Officer. Why, have you been robbed?

Mohr. On the contrary, I have found money!

Officer. Found money! where, when, how much?

Mohr. A one dollar note here in the street, I am terribly conscientious and though it is but one dollar, it would burn on my soul were I to keep it, even should I know a millionaire had lost it.

Officer. You're indeed an honest man!

Mohr. That is due to the spirit of the times. Take it in your care, and if nobody claims it, give it to the poor. [gives it.]

Officer. Who are you, and where do you come from?

Mohr. I am Max Hartfeld of Delphi, here are my recommendations. [gives letter which he received from Max.]

Officer. [Reads and returns it] All well! How long will you remain?

Mohr. That depends on circumstances; I have a lading of wool to dispose of.

Officer. On business then!

Mohr. I am.—We are now in an era of unparalelled corruption and laxity of the public conscience, but I strive to live honest.

Officer. The multitude lead such lives, but entirely *destitute* of honor.

Mohr. Yes, I have experienced that; even now there is a certain *fellow* here, who has the audacity to call himself Max Hartfeld.

Officer. Indeed!

Mohr. Contracts debts on my name and indulges in all manners of rascality.

Officer. He will be watched.

Mohr. Besides he possesses the peculiarity of feigning the most ignorant blockhead.

Officer. He shall not deceive me! — Does he bear any resemblance to your honor?

Mohr Not in the least. No comparison. He appears as though he were stuffed with cornmeal and roast beef—

Officer. Enough! If I ever detect him in my quarters, he shall be safely stored.—Adieu, my friend, should you at any time find money again, am always ready to receive it. [Exit.]

Mohr. [Contemptibly] Indeed!—Ha, ha, ha! Orpheus was noted for his beautiful lyrical airs; but I'll wager he threw a bribe into the jaws of that hell-hound, which made him tame and tractable as a lamb —I hope I have prepared a suitable bath for his corpulency, the groom. Now to counsel with my wife; for roguish tricks without womans cunning, are unpolished. [Exits.]

TABLEAU II.

Aurora's private apartment in DeRuyter's College. Elegantly furnished. C D backed by interiors. Piano R. Chairs, Tete-a tete L. Table L. Chair L of C D that will break down. Lapdog asleep on sofa. Vase and rosebush and drawings on table L.— Jayen playing on violin accompanied by Aurora with piano, discovered. Aurora strikes discord, Jayen grows impatient and crosses to C.—

Jayen. Confound that stupid idiot, Dutchman, he's likely to appear at any moment.

Aurora. Why what is the matter Jayen, you are unusually impatient to-day?

Jayen. Oh, I don't know! [aside] I'm going crazy—Come now your dancing lesson!

Aurora. I will not dance to-day, 'twill excite me too much —I am nervous.

Jayen. [Aside] Ah, yes, the arrival of the groom puts her all in a flurry.—Aurora, come here!

Aurora. What is it, Jayen?

Jayen. Are you content to share your fortunes and future joy and happiness with Max Hartfeld?

Aurora. Ah yes, willing and content! Tis the will of my poor dead mother; for on her deathbed she summoned me to her side, and grasping me with her cold hands, she said: "Alas, my poor child, I must leave you now, remember the little prayer I have always taught you, love your neighbor as yourself, and never— never betray your honor." Then placing my hand into a dear friend's who stood at her bedside, she continued to him: " Be thou ever a friend and protector to my child, promise to make her, yours"--that man was Max Hartfeld, this he did. Then bidding us to kneel at her side, she raised her aged hand and blessed us both--and in that blessing there is a future, never to cease happiness—and saying: "Now can I die content; soon will I be in the land of promise, in whose glory we may all some day repose, where all is bright; where no storm beats, and the unclouded sky shines on its own brightness." A last sigh—and I was an orphan. --I will now, in obedience, fulfill my mother's last wish! 'Twere more profitable for you to count the numberless stars, than to waste your affections on me. I must, I will obey my mother.

Servant appears at C D.

Servant. There is a gentleman in the parlor, says Aurora is his bride and desires to see her!

Aurora. Tis he, send him up immediately! [exit servant. Aurora runs to piano]

Jayen. Aurora, do not torture me thus; say that. you love me!

Aurora. Certainly I do—I love everybody; 'tis a Christian's principle--'twas my beloved mother's daily prayer. But, the love that I bear *him*, will make me happy, and to-day--my birthday-he comes to claim my hand.

Jayen. You have told me that three weeks ago.' But, consider me, a handsome and shapely young man, while he—

Aurora. Is preferable to you. He is a good soul, only a little awkward, and not acquainted with the customary usages of society and etiquette.--but I will cultivate him; and anent that, he possesses virtues which *you* cannot boast of. [Aurora plays. Max has been conducted on by servant who immediately exits again. Max sits on chair which breaks down. Aurora screams, rises and sees Max on floor. She looks at Jayen a moment in embarrassment.]

Max. Ha, ha, ha! dat shair he set me down!--Helle Aurora how you vas?

Aurora. Why Max what did you do?

Max. Oh pooty low; how vas you?

Aurora. You sat down too rudely and have broken the chair!

Max. Well you kno, dats my fashion. Mr. Figolinns, wen you blease shtand me up?

Jayen. With pleasure. [Plays on violin.]

Max. Wat you do mit dat fiddle, I vas no danzbear!

Jayen. Not? I beg your pardon! [delighted]

Aurora. [Has assisted him to rise] Mr. Faul, I am pleased to present you to Mr. Hartfeld; Mr. Hartfeld, this is Mr. Faul!

Max. Is it?—Well I don't kno him. [Walks L upsetting flowerpot on Aurora's drawing]

Aurora. [Crosses, takes drawing and goes to C] You monster, you soiled my drawing, you are terrible awkward!

Max. Well you kno Aurora, dat's my fashion.

Aurora. I want you to be more careful after this, and look where you are going.

Jayen. [Distinctly] That's right Aurora, pepper him!

Max. [Eyes Jayen]

Aurora. What's this, there's blood upon it?

Max. Vell, down shtairs in de barlor dere was a green robin on a shtick—I never see a robin like dat mit my life--he toll me he want some grackers; he dot I vas tame un I gif him mine paw, ewer dat rascal he bite me. I hauled off un hit em one--I tell you I don't bite me not any no more.

Aurora. He speaks of my parrot--I hope you have not killed it! [Rushes off C D]

Max. Wen de cats don't take em avay, he vas dere yet.--Se wat you maken here mit dat figolin?

Jayen. [Aside] I'd like to tell him something!--I am Miss Aurora's private instructor—

Max. Vat, you shtruck Aurora---

Jayen. No, no, I am teaching her to sing, dance and play.

Max. Oh, is dat so! he, he, he! Well I like dat, ha, ha, ha!

Re-enter Aurora.

Aurora. How unfortunate I am! You cruel wretch, you have murdered my pet. [Drops on chair]

Max. Aurora mine dear. don you gry, I gif you some pigeons wat laugh all de time—laughen pigeons you kno, ye e-s! dey bin tame un dont bite so much like dat dem robins!

Aurora. (Jumps up) What robin? 'Twas a parrot!

Max. A pair! no sir, I only make dat one dead.

Aurora. (Impatiently) No! I said it was a parrot, my favorite domestic pet.

Max. In bed! wen I hit em, he vas on a shtick.

Aurora. Oh, I could scratch your eyes out!

Jayen. (To Aurora) That's right, a little *more* pepper.

Aurora. There, that will do, leave us, go about your business. (Goes to Max, he embraces her.)

Max. Ah, Aurora, you bin a goot gerl un I love you. To-day vas your birthday, don't it? Ah, I don't forgot em, un I makes you un bresent.

Aurora. Yes, my poor mother—may she rest — set forth this day which makes you mine. Dear Max I love you!

Max. Now dat word makes me happiness. (Kisses her, looks at Jayen L again, but he has crossed to R. Max then looks R) Ha, ha, ha! dat's right, *a little more peffer!* — Aurora, you makes me some musid on dat—on dat—Clavier.

Aurora. With the greatest delight. (Runs to piano) Come here Max, sit beside me!

Max. (Goes to sit, but is afraid of breaking another chair, looks at the one he *has* broken) I-I sooner shtand me. (Sees Jayen's hat on piano, tries it on)

Jayen. Beg your pardon, that's my hat.

Max. Oh, he wont shteal me.

Jayen. (Takes his hat and goes to C D) Curses on him! But I'll have some satisfaction, I'll teaze him a trifle, he's silly enough to do anything I may challenge him.—Are you a good marksman?

Max. Don you see I vas, you dink I bin a shild?

Jayen. I w'll place my hand on this table—so, can you give it a severe blow and not miss the mark?

Max. I can do dat, un you never find et oud. (Blows on Jayen's hand)

Jayen No, no, strike with your hand.

Max. Wy don you say so. (Strikes at Jayen's hand, he withdraws it and Max strikes the table. Jayen laughs. Max vexedly imitates him and seizes Jayen by the neck) You laugh me oud, I shoke you. (Shakes him) Wat vor you make me dat foolishness?—You dink a Dutchman is a geese?

Jayen. *I was only joking!*

Max. Vas you, so vas I! (Shakes him again then throws him off) How you like dat? Shtick et in your pocket, un wen you loose em, comes back I gif you some more.

Jayen. You monster—

Max. *Oh, I vas only shoken!*

Jayen. You've almost strangled me.

Max. Vell you kno, dat's my fashion.

Jayen. He has a grip like a vice! (Going to c d) Never mind, I'll be even with you yet; I'll meet you again, and, by heaven, I'll *tear* you to pieces. (Rushes off C D)

Max. Come back here oder I turn you outside in—dat feller he ran like blixen.

Aurora. (Leads him to front) I want to tell you something—if Madam—

Max. Wat's de use dat feller—uf he dont look oud I meet him un I—

Aurora. Never mind that now, listen to me—

Max. Wat's de use dat feller make me dat foolishness un hit me on de dable! Oo-oo—it was a goot ding he gone out oder I tear *l'm* mit pieces.

Aurora. Listen to me!—If Madam DeRuyter should chance to come in this room, make yourself agree ble, be careful of what you do, don't be awkward and commit another mischief remember. I want to cultivate and introduce you in society. (Chuckles him under the chin) You will do this, I know you will and then I will kiss you.

Max. Vell, you can do *dat* right avay.

Aurora. Sh! she comes.

Enter Madam DeRuyter.

(Aurora runs to meet her, brings her to c, calls Max, he turns awkwardly and against DeRuyter.)

DeRuyter. Ah, Mr. Hartfeld, you are most welcome! Aurora. did you give your intended consort a suitable reception?

Aurora. (Courtseying to Max) Most assuredly I did. (Taps him on cheek, bows and crosses)

Max. (Heartily imitates her, almost falling) Wat's de matter on you, (to DeRuyter) you bin not well? Wy don you vas like me?—You come in Delphi onced, in de country, wen I bin dere it mine Aurora, un in four weeks I send you home so fat like de geese von de shtoppels. (Aurora retires, blushing with shame)

DeRuyter. I am extraordinarily obliged to you. (Crosses. Aside) Faults of ignorance are excusable.—Sit down and be comfortable.

Max. (Looks at broken chair then front of himself on floor) I t n afraid on dat shairs!

DeRuyter. Then be seated on the sofa.

Max. Well dat's so! I will do dat. (Sits on sofa l. on DeRuyter's lapdog sleeping there, who squeaks) Wat vas dat squeak en?

DeRuyter. For heaven's sake, I hope you've not sat on my Franchette!

Max. No sir! who vas your Franchette?

DeRuyter My lapdog! My sweet pet! Get up, you monster, get up I say!

Max Hold on, dat done gone so fast. (Brings small dog out, holding it up looks at it) Dat's so, one little dog-beast! (Drops it) Sticks all fours out.

DeRuyter. (Takes it up) Dead!—Oh, I wish you were in the loneliness of the Great Desert!

Max. Wat I make dere?

DeRuyter. He is dead, my idol, my all!

Max. Cst be quiet, I gif you one wat vas five times bigger as dat.

DeRuyter. You are a dolt, sir, a barbarous dolt!

Max I don't kno wat at vas. In Delphi de dogs don't shleep on de sofa.

DeRuyter. That will do! Don't drive me to madness.—These precious remains! I will take you out of sight of this heartless miscreant; bedew you with my tears, and curse the murderer who has robbed me of my joy forever! (Exit)

Max. (Rises, watches her off) Dat womans talk ust like a book.

Aurora. Max, come here!

Max. Wat you vant?

Aurora. Now that we are alone, I must tell you, that, you behaved in the most disagreeable manner.

Max. Yaw mine Gott in Himmel, wat have I do?

Aurora You have been bungling extremely again. I told you to be careful, and despite that, you crushed my mistress' lapdog.

Max. Well you kno dat's my fashion.

Aurora. Well but you know, I want you to wean that fashion.

Max. Well dat's so. You vas—oh, you vas only shoken?

Aurora. No, I mean what I say.

Max. You vas mad on me den?

Aurora. Don't say *mad*, but *angry*.

Max. Ye-es, I vas hungry, I bin—

Aurora. You misunderstood me. When you are, as you term it, *mad*, you must say, I am angry.

Max. Well I don't kno ut you vas engry, dat's de reason wat vor I ask you.

Aurora. Oh, no, but your present ways and habits must be broken. I take great interest in you and will exercise you every day

Max. Aurora you bin a goot gerl, I love you!

Aurora. And I love you in return.

Max. To-day vas your birthday un I bring one bresent vor you, von Delphi. You kno wat at vas?

Aurora. No!

Max. (Gives her a paper) Here is un sheck on de Bank of Delphi, for five-dousand dollars, dat vas all yours.

Aurora. A present of five thousand dollars? (Opens, looks at it)

Jayen. [Appears at C D]

Max. Dat's wat I toll you, ust look on dat bapers.

Aurora. Are you telling me a falsehood, or--

Max. Wat, Aurora! mine dear Mutter she always say, " Max, never tell a lie"--you dink I toll you somedings den wat was not so?

Aurora. Then do you pretend to call this a bank check?

Max. Ye-e-s, dat vas--no, I vas a mistake ha, ha, ha! (Examines other papers and pockets) I show you!--I believe I loose me dat sheck!--J don kno how dat vas--I don't loose em, dat's a shoor ding—hold on I find em! (Gets his hat and goes to c D. Jayen disappears) Aurora, I gone away, I dink I make one mistake un gif dat sheck to mine servant, un I don't kno dat. (Exit Max—Jayen appears—Max returns—Jayen disappears) Aurora, I will find him un I comes back right away. (Kisses her) Goot bye! (Exits—Jayen re-appears—re-enter Max—Jayen again disappears) Aurora, now I dink on it. I lay me dat sheck on dis table—no! Don't bin alone, I comes back right avay, goot bye! Exit—Jayen returns, runs to piano, takes his violin, which he had forgotten, when Max re-enters again) Aurora, it vas a goot ding dat feller mit at figolin was gone ond right away, oder—(sees Jayen who is about to exit with his violin, Max brings him down) Hold on I show you somedings! (Takes violin and hauls off, Jayen dodges him as the violin descends, the momentum throwing Max to the floor—Comic position— Jayen at door triumphant— Aurora stands amazed—Tableau—Quick drop.

ACT II. TABLEAU III.

Scene I. Street—Dr. Phaeton's Insane Asylum with practicable door Ignatius discovered knocking at door, which is opened by Dr. Phaeton in dressing gown.

Mohr. I desire to see Dr. Phaeton.

Doctor. 'Tis he who now addresses you.

Mohr. I have heard of your efficiency in the curing of lunatics; do you make that a specialty?

Doctor. Yes sir! and I have had the good fortune of restoring scores of them back to society again. My practice is confined chiefly, to the quiet insanity of a fixed idea : who imagine they are persons of distinction and the like How can I serve you? Do you perhaps feel such paroxisms too ?

Mohr. No sir, not I! but my uncle, my poor uncle, the family of Linden may be known to you ?

Doctor: I don't remember such a name.

Mohr. My uncle, Mr. Linden has had the misfortune to lose his good senses ; he imagines he is a farmer by the name of Max Hartfield. He was quiet at that for a time, but now he has fixed it in his head that he is a bridegroom—escaped, and ran straight-forward into the city to be married, consequently, we concluded to subject him to your treatment

Doctor: Certainly. Send him to me under some pretext:

Mohr. We shall—I will pay you partly in advance (pays him money.)

Doctor. Bring him immediately, the sooner—the better.

Mohr. In ten minutes he will be in your care. (exit Doctor.) Excellent! The Doctor will lock him up for two or three days at least: affording me ample time to take my wife to Delphi—now for the *crazy* man. (Advances right when enterr Max.) Why Max, what is the matter, you seem so ardent?

Max. I bin so glad I find you mine dear! I got one sheck for five dousand dollars, un I lose me dat sheck, dink I gif *you* dat sheck mid at unner bapers.

Mohr. No Max, there was but one paper in the envelope you gave me and that I have disposed of, according to your order. But Max, you look very bad, you are not well.

Well, it was no wonder ust now, wen I die right away. Ef I only kno were dat sheck was. Aurora will gone mad on me—she dink I toll her she was a liar!

Mohr. (aside) Very probably she will! Leave that to me, I will find it if you have lost it here. But you look terrible bad indeed, take my advice and go to some Doctor.

Max. Ye-e-s, dat big drubles—un I bin so hungry, wen I vas a bull I don't shtand em.

Mohr. Therefore! Fortunately there is a Doctor right here, go to him and let him prescribe for you.

Max. May be he sharge me too many?

Mohr. Oh no, Max, it's a free—State Institution, all for the sake of humanity.

Max. Well mine dear servant, den I will do dat. When you find me dat sheck—(pushing at door.)

Mohr. I will bring it to you, certainly (aside) I won't. Knock at the door!

Max. Well dat's so. (knocks.)

Mohr. You may wait in there till I return (aside), but that will never be.

Max. Shoor, and den me gone eaten somedings. (door opens,) adam enters, pushes Max away from the door, runs forward, cutting capers. Max turns, flourishing his fists in door.) You comes back here, order I—(Adam pushes him in quickly and follows.)

Mohr. Ha, ha, ha! Tis a pity that I cannot witness the ensuing scene, but, I have different petty matters to attend to and must be off. (exit in haste.)

SCENE II.

Room in Dr. Phaeton's Asylum. Min Cutts in Kingly attire and crown on head, and Lank, both seated—discovered. Max is shoved on by Adam.

Adam. Here is company for you. The Doctor will be here directly. (Exit)

Max. (Looks at the lunatics who are perfectly motionless) Dem fellers dont say nottings—he dont move his eyes—ha, ha, ha! dey don kno I vas here. He got one cap on his head, wat look so much like king David, wat I see in de bible. Maybe dey vas only doll-babies, I find em out! (Advances to Lank)

Lank. (Shouts) Don't come too near me!

Max. Vor wat for?

Lank. Don't you see that I am of glass?

Max. Von gless?

Lank. Yes sir, and of the finest quality!

Max. Is dat possible!—Vell it wouldn't vas a pad idea wen all de beoples vas von gless, den we see dat pad blood a-a-gone round so much—circuliren. But I dink you vas pooty dim gless. (Looks at him closely)

Lank. For heaven's sake I say, don't come too near me!

Max. Alright!—Den I gone to dis feller. (Nearing Min Cutts)

Cutts. (Harshly) Keep at a distance!

Max. You vas von gless too?

Cutts. I am King Cambyses of Persia; I have conquered Egypt!

Max. You—is dat so! Well I dink you vas -

Cutts. Slave, down on your knees, or I will crush thee!

Max. I begs your bardon, dat vas too hard on me.

Cutts. You shall be a highpriest of Isis!

Max. No sir, no humbuck! I bin a goot gristian (Aside) I wonder wat vor kind beoples is dat?—Here vas dat feller wat bring me in.

Enter Adam, dives to C.

Adam. The Doctor will be here soon!

Max. (Taking Adam aside) Who vas dem fellers dere?

Adam. Poor unfortunates who have lost their senses.

Max. Crazy?

Adam. And are under the treatment of Doctor Phaeton.

Max. Well I dink we bet'er gone outside den.

Adam. Never fear, they are entirely harmless. We may thank God that we still retain our good senses.

Max. Ye e-s!—Dank God!

Adam. He was disappointed in love, and now imagines he is of glass.

Max. Dat's wat he toll me.

Adam. And he was formerly a powerful fanatic, blasphemy and affrontery were his daily prayers, and finally his brain became unsettled.

Max. He toll me he vas de King von Persien.

Adam. Probably he is, but not King Cambyses, he cannot be, because his father, King Cyrus needs first must know it, and this King Cyrus is myself! (Strides towards Max)

Max. (Starts—aside) Here is an unner dam fool!—You—you
va King Cyrup? I dot you vas a monkey on a shtick!
Adam. (Majestically stepping toward Max) Did you not re-
cognize my *Majesty* immediately?
Max. (Retiring near Lank) No sir, I bin *his* master.
Lank! Don't come too near me!
Max. Mine gootness, nein!
Adam. I have made King Croesus my prisoner.
Max. He gif you one bresent? Is dat so!
Adam. The Babylonian Jews I privileged to return to their
homes.
Max. Ye-e-s, I gone home ter-morrow! (Still backed by Adam
Max nears Cutts)
Cutts. Keep at a distance!
Max. Mine gootness, I believe I vas in a mad house!

Enter Doctor Phaeton.

Max. You vas de Doctor?
Doctor. I am.
Max. I bin gled you vas here. Wat you make mit all dem
grazy fools here?
Doctor. Do you wish to be acquainted with them?
Max. No sir; I dink I kno dem pooty well now.
Doctor. May I ask your name?
Max. I vas Max Hartfeld von Delphi; I got one bride here wat
I take home mit myself, un den I gone married.
Doctor. Yes, yes! I know it all. Adam, get the key of No. 16
and bring it to me. The bars at the door and window are in a
good condition?
Adam. They are. (Exit)
Max. Wat—you gone lock me up un shtick me in?
Doctor. I generally begin cautiously with patients under your
circumstances
Max. Dances—wat for kind dances?
Doctor. Where fixed ideas have taken root, we must be serious.
Max. Mine Gott in Himmel, I vas de honest Max Hartfeld von
Del—
Doctor. (Serious) You tell me that for the last time. You are
Mr. Linden, you see—*I know you.*
Max. I vas Mr. Linden! (Aside) I believe dat feller vas grazy
too!—I wonder where de Doctor vas--I must gif in oder he gone
mad.
Doctor. Well sir, who are you?
Max. (Friendly) Mr. Linden, certainly.

Re-enter Adam with key.

Adam. The key of No. 16.
Doctor. Now Mr. Linden, follow me!
Max. Vat?

Doctor. *Follow me!*

Max. (Aside) Maybe he dink I vas a dam fool too!—Wen you blease Doctor—you vas de Doctor?

Doctor. Certainly I am.

Max. De Doctor of King Cambyses?

Adam. [Strides to Max and taps him on shoulder] Of King Cyrus!

Max. Well dat's so! You see I vas not goot for dis shentle combany. I vas only un farmer, Max Hart—

Doctor. [Threatening[Who are you, whom?

Max. Mr. Linden, shoor! [Aside, going to door] I drimbles all over.

Doctor. Where are you going?

Max. I gone outside un hunt mine Shpitten Devil.

Doctor. You will not leave this place. You are entrusted to my care.

Max. No sir, I dont care. I vas not well, I get some pad blood [aside] after while.—You gif me un proscription, I gif you sixteen cent.

Doctor. In the first weeks I don't prescribe, but only observe.

Max. Wat, you dink I shtay here two oder dree weeks?

Doctor. At least two or three months.

Max. You dink I shtay here two oder dree months, were de lunadics vas all over de blace?—Mine bustness, you kno I vas a farmer—

Doctor. What are you, what are you?

Max. Well, de hole world knows dat I vas Mr. Linden. Awer Auro mine bride—

Doctor. You have no bride.

Max. Vat—well dat's so!

Doctor. You must dismiss that from your mind also. And now, save all further conditions—march to No. 16.

Lank. March!

Cutts. March!

Max. [Aside] Now it vas time I gone oud!

Doctor Well, well I

Max. [Still aside] Knifes un bishtols dem fools dont got, un mine dogs—[Meaning his fists]

Doctor. What, are you murmuring?

Max. I fix em!—Doctor un all your Kings, goot bye! [Advances to door]

Doctor. Adam stop him! [Adam stands front of door]

Max. [Shakes Doctor by the neck and forces him to sit down on floor]

Doctor. Cutts and Lank seize him! [Cutts merely rises and assumes dramatic attitude and points to C of stage—Lank steals to door—Adam attacks Max, when Max throws him against Lank who is about to exit]

TABLEAU IV.

Scene I.—Sitting room in the "Little Globe Hotel" — Table and Chairs R, also L—Call bell on table.

Enter Max and Ignatius Mohr.

Max. No sir, mine dear serwant, I dont like dis town, Indianapolis. In Delphi, de cows un oxes gone out my way wen I comes past, un here—de fellers mit wheelbarrows runs me over un de mooles un shakass dey whisper in mine ears; I don like dat.—Awer se, vor wat vor you send me in dat dog-gone madhouse?

Mohr. Why, Doctor Phaeton is one of the most renowned physicians in all Indianapolis!

Max. Ye-e-s, awer I dont see dat Doctor at all—all grazy beoples, King Cyrup, King Cambyses, one feller von gless un some unner dam fool, wat all times say I vas Mr. Linden, ye-e-s!

Mohr. [Hypocritically smiling] Probably the Doctor was not at home You may wait about fifteen minutes and—

Max Un den I gone in again? You dink I vas grazy too? No sir, I bin gled I vas oud!—You find me dat sheck? [Sits at table]

Mohr. Not yet, Max! don't worry about that check, I'll find—I will inquire—

Max. I dont care many vor dat sheck, awer you see, wen I comes back un tell Aurora I dont got at sheck, she will toll me I fool her un I vas a liar! I don like dat.

Mohr. [Aside] But precisely I *do!*

Max: Un wen you dont find at sheck soon, pooty quick. I tell de Telegraph office, un he gone in Delphi, on de Saving Bank, ust like blixen un shtop de bayment von dat sheck.

Mohr. [Aside] Indeed ! that is, provided I give you an opportunity

Max. I bin so hungry as I never was before!

Mohr. You may order anything you desire—here. [Taps call bell]

Max. Maybe dey sharge me too many?

Mohr. Not one cent—it is just luncheon time!

Max. Alright, I eat me some lunch—awer I dont see nobody wat gif me somedings.

Mohr. The waiter will be here directly.

Enter Oakdale Dawsillet.

Mohr. [Aside to Oakdale] Give that man anything he may call for, he'll pay all. [To Max] Mr. Dawsillet will serve you; meanwhile Max, I will make diligent search for your check. [Aside, going] The wind blows in a different direction now and I must change my tac tics again.—You will stop the payment of that check will you! we shall see—I have it. I will instruct my wife, she must pursue and inveigh him for a breach of affiance, undoubtedly he will be placed under a few days' arrest, And if the wieldy Jayen Faul dips his spoon into the affair, he will fall into a snare, so cunningly laid by me for his unwary feet, that would confound and dismay him. [Exit]

Max. Well, wat for you shtand here? [Oakdale starts] I want somedings wat I eat!

Oakdale. Oh, certainly, I run, I fly fast as the wind to serve you. [Exit]

Max. Well, dat's a funny feller; de wind dont fly—wen he say de wind *mill*, yes, dey got *wings*, dey fly! Dat's wat de beoples say, I don kno, I never see one fly mit my whole life.

Re enter Oakdale with eight small saucers.

Oakdale. Here are eight portions, you have your choice.

Max. Alright! [Looks at them astonished] Now ust look on dem blates! dat was de salats, dont it? Now you brings de polony un sauerkraut?

Oakdale. I beg your pardon, that is all!

Max. Dat vas all? You dink I vas a shicken?

Oakdale. Oh no! I do not venture to compare you with any fowl or bird whatever.

Max. Wen I vas on de table, I eat so many like a bear—dont forgot et! [Eats]

Oakdale. Perhaps the gentleman wishes some wine?

Max. Ye·e s, de best wat you got! [Aside] Et dont cost noddings.

Oakdale. Our wines are all excellent, direct from the best vaults; Rudesheimer, Frontigna, Wuerzburg, Madeira, Catawba, Concord, Burgundy, Hauthbrion, Cantor, Claret, Mayence, De La-Rhue, Porteau, Rhenish—

Max. [Places hand on Oakdale's mouth] Mine gootness keep quiet ef you blease! Give me some Wuerzburg, dat gro in Shermany, you know I like dat.

Oakdale. [Going] Yes sir!

Max. He! Mr. Somebody, let em blates gone mit you.

Oakdale. Shall I fill them again?

Max.. Shoor, wat else? [Exit Oakdale with plates] I don kno I eat me somedings, I only taste em one little bit, un den it vas all.

Leona appears at C D, backed on by Ignatius who holds a revolver to her head.

Mohr. [To Leona, at back] You shall be watched; remember what I have told you, or—[Putting the weapon, disappears]

Leona. [Recollecting, comes forward] Ah, I am just in time: you are alone!

Max. I don kno, don you vas nobody?

Leona. Man loves company, though 'tis only a burning taper, said a certain famous writer.

Max. I don kno who dat vas.

Leona. May I have the honor to entertain you awhile?

Max. Wen I eat, I dont hear many.

Re-enter Oakdale.

Oakdale. Eight fresh portions!

Max. Eight fresh mouthfuls, why don you say!—Well, where vas dat wine?

Oakdale. Beg your pardon, I forgot all about it. [Exit, Max eats]

Leona. [Gets chair and sits left of Max] I will endeavor to interest you with a little romance.

Max. I got no time. [Eating]

Leona. Do they not impress your nerves?

Max. I got no nerves.

Leona. But a feeling for the beautiful—

Max. Oh ye-e s!

Leona. Ah, happy is he, to whom this sensibility, nature has not endowed with excess. If my fate were known to you—

Max. No sir, I dont kno!

Leona. My name is Amelena Moss! [Drawing nearer]

Max. Is dat so?

Leona. I was young and sprightly, the delight of my parents, when, unfortunately, one day, I was enjoying a sylvan jollity in Delphi—[Is close by his side at this time]

Max. (Turns head suddenly, bringing his face in contact with Leona) In Delphi?

Leona. Are you acquainted there?

Max. Ye-e-s I vas, ha, ha, ha! I live dere!

Leona. I became associated with a young man, his name was Max Hartfeld—

Max. Max Hartfeld!

Leona. He was exceedingly handsome; vanquished my heart, accepted my hand; and swearing everlasting fidelity, he promised me to marry—

Max. Se Miss Annelena, dat vas not so!

Leona. Alas! It is only too true!

Max. (Aside) I believe dat poor womans dont feel well—You better take mine advice un gone down mit at Doctor in de lunatic sylum.

Leona. The cruel man, he has deserted his promise!

Max. You don kno wat you say. In de whole Delphi dere vas only *one* Max Hartfeld, un dat vas *me!*

Leona. What, you—you are my Max—

Max. No sir, not your's, I vas mine. (Rises)

Leona. (Has risen, regards him closely) Ah yes! I remember the charming features that captivated my heart; the rosy cheeks; the sparkling countenance; the voice, and stout as ever—yes, yes, you *are* my Max! (Backs him)

Max. (Folding arms, imitates Lank) Dont come too near me! I never see you mit my life!

Leona. How inhuman! even now you dare deny it, now, when destiny, peradventure, so remarkably brings us confront?

Max. Wat, bin net si rab bat si &c.—I dont undershtand one word wat she say. Gone away—dont make my head warm.

Leona. Such are men, when their hearts grow cold, their heads become warm. (Fiercely toward him) But fear my wrath, my vengeance—(Drops on chair) Oh, the barbarian, I love him yet!

Max. Dat womans vus grazy. When I vas not only mit her mineself! Dank God! here vas dat shentlemans!

Oakdale returns with wine.

Oakdale. Your wine sir! (Leona whispers him)

Leona. In my veins there is a glowing fire! (Draws dagger) Give me peace of heart and mind or tremble!

Max. (Defends with chair) Wen I dont look outside, dat womans she make me dead. (Keeps his eyes fixed on Leona)

Leona. Tyrant of my heart! At the sight of you I feel as though I had swallowed balls of fire!

Max. Mishter, wen·you blease, gif me mine hat—put em on mine head—I must watch dat grazy womans, till I vas outside mit at door.

Oakdale. First, the gentleman will please pay the *carte payante.*

Max. I dont need no cards, I never blay mit my life.

Leona. But cruelly you have played a game with my heart!

Oakdale. Sir, I mean the bill.

Max. For wat for, I only eat me some lunch.

Oakdale. What, lunch! we charge for luncheons here. Sixteen portions, one bottle of the best German wine—sum substance, four dollars.

Max. Ye-e-s, I gif you one kick four times, dat's wat I do—don you vas ashame! you dink I got enough!

Oakdale. That's not my fault, I can't help that.

Leona. Dear Max! when you are in danger, fly to my arms and seek protection.

Max. Gone away I toll you!

Oakdale. I will retain your hat, 'till you have paid me.

Max. Dat vas too funny! I gone oud un find mine Shpitten Devil—

Oakdale. Don't leave this place, or—

Leona. My fury will awake! (Raising dagger)

Max. You bandits! wen you comes here, I hit you in de mouth mit at shairs, you never grack any nuts no more mit your life. (Throws chair front of door and exits—Oakdale runs, falls over chair—Leona drops dagger and laughs heartily—Scene closes in.)

Scene II.—Street in Indianapolis.

Enter Ignatius Mohr.

Mohr. He comes this way—I must not loose sight of him. (Retires)

Enter Max, looking off, when he sees Ignatius who is coming forward.

Max. Ach mine dear Shpitten Devil, here you vas! toll me wat I make, wat I do!

Mohr. Why did you not get anvthing to eat?

Max. Not so much as one bullfrog.—Dere vas some grazy beoples wat run me after un murder me.

Mohr. Murder you! why—

Max. Ye-e-s, I toll you dat after wile, ust come on now!

Mohr. Where is your hat?

Max. Never mind mine hat—you better toll me where mine head was, I don kno where he shtand.

Enter Oakdale and Leona.

Oakdale. Here he is, you dare not run away now!

Leona. Yes barbarian, you shall not escape me!

Max. No, dat makes me too many trubles.

Mohr. (Aside) I'll be scarce and observe at a distance. (Exit, patting his revolver to Leona as threatening)

Oakdale. The *carte payante*, sir—

Leona. My innocence, my heart!

Max. Se, wen you make mine head mad, I holler fire! un all de beoples from de blace comes right here.

Oakdale. You will pay me first, then cry out so long as suits your pleasure.

Leona Alas, my heart has no price! (Approaching Max, who avoids her)

Max. Help! Diefs! Murder! Fire, fire, fi—

Enter Bells Gap the officer—Leona crosses.

Officer. What parvenu is this, what means this alarm?

Max. Ach mine dear sir, I vas a shtranger here un I bin surrounded mit a band robbers.

Officer. Fear nothing, sir,—What mean you, what would you with this man?

Oakdale. I served him sixteen portions of choice delicacies with the best wine, and now he refuses to pay me!

Leona. To me he has broken a promise and deserted me. (Retires and eventually steals off)

Max. Dam lies!

Officer. Indeed! Sir, these are various ill reproofs. Inasmuch as you are a stranger here and of quite a respectable appearance, you will be treated with lenity. Who are you, and where do you come from?

Max. I vas Max Hartfeld von Delphi!

Officer. Aha! so you are *that* precious bird! 'Tis well—I know you now.

Max. I bin so gled I find somebody now, wat kno who I vas!

Officer. I express my satisfaction and thanks, that you have pursued this scoundrel, this swindler.

Max. Wat shwindler! Mine gootness, nobody never shwindel me!

Officer. You are nothing less than Max Hartfeld. 'Tis scarcely three hours since I met with the noble possessor of that name—who is an honest, benevolent and trustworthy man.—You are an impostor under an assumed name.—Come along!

Max. Potz donner und alle hagel! now you toll me dat I vas not even dat shennine Max Hartfeld?

Officer. (Abruptly) No!

Max! After wile ago I vas mineself, un now you toll me dat I vas somebody else—I dont see how dat vas! (Coolly going R) I dont undershtand me dat!

Officer. One moment, please!

Max. One moment—alright!—Dat vas one moment. (Resumes advancing, officer again stays him) Wat you vant? (Brings his head in contact with officer's nose)

Officer. Permit me to ask you, have you any letters, papers of recommendation or the like, to prove your name?

Max. Ye-e-s, shoor! I was—

Officer! Let me see them, please!

Caracelli. (Off stage) Statoots-a, vases, statoots-a!

Max. (Searches pockets, looks for his servant Ignatius) Mine servant he vas here ust now, un now he vas not here—well he gif em to de Police Office.

Officer. You lie—I did not—

Max. No sir, I shtand!

Officer. An indigent excuse, which I cannot accept.—You must go with me to the lockup.

Max. Wat I make dere?

Officer. That you shall learn, only too soon. Where are you going?

Max. I call me dat France womans wat I kill dat dog mit; she toll you I vas mineself.

Officer. No prevaricatio is now! I'll hear—none. Come along.

Max. No sir, I dont!

Oakdale. Yes sir, you will!

Max. I don care when you vas a dossen fellers! — Come on! (Officer and Oakdale seize him. Max with one sling is free, he presses Officer and Oakdale together, face to face, which forces them to embrace each other, and throws them against Caracelli the image vender, who has just entered. All fall, breaking Caracelli's images to atoms.

Caracelli. A thousand devils, my busts, my statoots-a!

Max. (Laughs heartily at the group on floor. Officer rises, catches Max again) You dont got enough yet? Wen you dont look out I shtand you downside up, (gesturing) like dat!

Officer. You must go with me, despite the devil. (Produces handcuffs)

Oakdale. That's right, that will bring him along!

Max. Is dat so!—well. uf I *must* gone along, den you blease carry me. (Sits down on floor. Officer whispers Caracelli pointing off L. Caracelli exit hastily L)

Officer. You will regret this, attacking me, an officer. Just sit there about two minutes only, I will cure you of some of your good humor, and we will see who is ahead then

Max. Sit down here, I toll you somedings. (Smiling)

Officer. No badinage now, I am serious!

Re-enter Caracelli with a canal-barrow.

Officer. Now if it pleases your independence, take a seat in that.

Max. Well, ust set me in, dat gif me some good exercises. (Aside) I fix em! (All three lift him in barrow—Officer goes to the shafts, Oakdale and Caracelli at the front purporting to pull) Now I vas in, when Aurora see me now, I wonder wat she toll me!— Hold on—hold on, I toll you hold on!

Officer. Keep quiet now, or—

Max. Dere vas a nail in dere, he shaggen me! (The bottom of wheelbarrow breaks through, Max goes down doubled up; he straightens out—forcing the barrow apart. Officer and the others seize him; he throws them off and takes one of the shafts of barrow and defends—swinging it right and left, lightly as a cane) Who vas ahead now! (Tableau! Quick drop)

ACT III. TABLEAU V.

Room in the "Little Globe Hotel," furnished ad libitum.—C D and R C D.—Table and chairs.—Occupied by Ignatius and Leona.

Leona enters C D as curtain rises.

Leona. I have stolen away unnoticed!—Poor man! to be the victim of my constrained imposition; to think, that through my machinations, forced upon me by my husband, he should be reproved by the minions of the law—almost rends my heart. But, a little patience yet, and I will atone for it, yes, yes! And if it comes to the worst I will battle for him, defend him and betray the real offender—and that is my husband, oh God! my husband, who forced me on to this, for what purpose I know not.—Yet, this is all a mere trifle aneut the most horrible crime of murder:—Hark! methinks he comes—Ah, how well I yet remember when first his voice lisped to me, but, alas, to-day that voice whispers seduction in secret, or thunders destruction at the head of a devoted wife! I would tell him, remember those sportive groups of youth, in whose halcyon bosoms there sleeps an ocean, as yet scarcely ruffled by the passions, which soon shall heave it as with a tempest's strength. Did I not devote, expend, consecrate myself to the holy work of his melioration; did I not dare to stand forth in his defense, when detraction was aiming it's deadly weapon at his reputation! But, without avail! How I loved him then—he loved me too. Oh, there were hours when I could hang forever on his brow, but time, which stole in silent swiftness by, strewed as he hurried on his path, with thorns. Now—now he does no longer acknowledge me with the same cordiality; does not treat me with the same friendly attention and gentleness, as when the claims of pride in honor and virtue, did not interfere with those of friendship! He will come and chide, rail and curse me, wake me from my dreams of *fate*, to blend his nascent grossness with my tears! (Sinks on chair, head on table)

Enter Jayen Faul C D

Jayen. (At door) Ah!

Leona. How timorous I feel!

Jayen. Pardon me, if I am intrusive.

Leona. (Rises and tries to conceal her tears—Aside) Jayen!—Certainly—certainly. (Aside) What brings him here!

Jayen. I came to speak to your husband, Ignatius Mohr, or as he now chooses to call himself, Edmund !

Leona. He is absent now, but methinks, sir, he will be here anon. (Still avoiding her countenance from Jayen)

Jayen. I have heard of things of which I would demand an explanation—but how is this, you are distracted, you have been weeping—your looks betray you! Did your husband perhaps—

Leona. Oh, no! I-I was only dreaming—dreaming of the days of yore, when you disturbed me.

Jayen. From that I infer you are not happy as once you have been. You will pardon me if I am wrong, for I, in part, suspect your husband to be at the bottom of this and what I know. What he once was he is not, and what he is now—heaven knows. If you tell me all, you will earn my lifelong gratitude.

Leona. (Aside) Betray my husband to one who is almost a stranger to me!

Jayen. Do you hesitate?

Leona. [Still aside] He must promise to keep it secret, for perhaps there may yet be some hope, some means left to save him; still I fear that I only hope against darkening despair. [To Jayen] 'Tis scarcely three hours since first we met, and our acquaintance is but ocular: yet, I will confide in you, if you promise to keep it all a secret and not to betray my husband?

Jayen. I promise!

Leona. Will you swear it ?

Jayen. I swear it !

Leona. Then listen to me, confide in him no more, lest you fall into a ditch—trenched by him—a victim of his treachery. Heaven forgive me saying this of my husband. My heart revolts against this desperate step I am taking, but my conscience tells me I am peaking the truth.

Jayen. None but a noble heart could speak thus!

Leona. He was a man of ability and promise when he married me; we were blithe and happy as mortals ere could be, and prosperous. But, as the fickle formed clouds come and pass away, so did our happiness. Reverse followed reverse and soon our fortunes were swept away with a hurricane swiftness, emergently placing him under the painful necessity of seeking employment. This was to him an austere task. Sauntering along to find it, day after day he eventually became acquainted with all sorts of vices imaginable; mingled with the lowest and vilest of all society, and under their influence wasted a splendid opportunity, to engage in an honest enterprise. Vice, succeeded virtue—corruption, honesty and misery, happiness. Depraved, he reveled in high gambling, wanton lechery and debauch; his innate wit waxed exceedingly arrant and thus he eked out an infecund life of infamy.

Jayen. Is it possible, that a man endowed with nature's rarest gifts, could fall to such a base degree of ignominy?

Leona. Ah that is not all; to further and succeed in his malignant designs, he made me an instrument of his crimes. Ha, I blush with shame while I owe it—but I suffered it all, hoping I could some day break his chain of iniquities and bring him safely back to the path of virtue. But now it cannot be, it is too late--too late! [Drops on chair]

Jayen. Poor creature!—and you are but a mere toy in the hands of your tempter, at whose door the sin and punishment of his crimes and cruelty belongs. Nevertheless, a part of the misery accruing to his crimes was to be yours—all innocent though you are at heart. Now I would ask you, why did he not come when I had written him and how did he dispose of the money I advanced him?

Leona. How! squandered it; lavished it in pursuance of his crimes and vices and things worse Never would he have obeyed your summons, but for the perpetration of—ha, I dare not mention it - and pursued with remorse and to escape justice and capital punishment, did he leave Chicago. Having a fit opportunity he came here to Indianapolis, solemnly swearing to begin a new life with a new name.

Jayen. A new name –traveled here afoot—I see it all. Now do I hold him the false and treacherous villain I suspected him to be. But a little patience yet, until his course becomes clearly defined, his object manifest, then—then it will be *my* turn. [Goes to Leona who sits at table concealing her face]

Ignatius appears and remains at door C.

Mohr. [Aside] Does she weep?

Jayen. He comes not! Adieu, fair lady! I will seek your husband and find him—

Mohr. [Comes down] Right here! It is I whom you seek I presume?

Leona rises, tries to conceal her grief.

Jayen. Decidedly yes, and more than that—a poignant interview.

Mohr. [Goes to Leona gently leading her to R I E] Leave us, my darling wife! until your presence will be again required.

Leona. [Surprised] Ah, how caressing he was! [Exit]

Mohr. Why, have you about four hundred and fifty dollars for me? Remember, your employee has earned them now.

Jayen. Listen to me pseudo Edmund! Though I possessed four hundred and fifty times four hundred and fifty dollars, I would not now give you the one four hundred and fiftieth part of a single dollar.

Mohr. [Surprised] Ah, indeed! [Aside] Why does he speak thus, can Leona have discovered to him—Jayen Faul! some malevolent mammal or other, has, with malice aforethought, deceived you and slandered me, or why do you thus speak meanly abrupt?

Jayen. No, not slandered by any one, but I have seen, heard and experience!—

Mohr. Cut that! I have served you and my requirements are conformably fulfilled, consequently it is due me now, and if you refuse it, I appeal to your honor.

Jayen. [Starting] Honor! You speak of honor! The boldest highway robber who roams at broad daylight, has more of honor, than the cowardly, stealthy hand that aims a blow in the dark, and leaves, like a poisoned serpent's fang, a sure and deadly mark! Fie!—where is my rival now, Max Hartfeld?

Mohr. He is safely provided for and will not interfere for a time at least.

Jayen. I want no assurances now, but facts. If you have no answer—I have.

Mohr. He was arrested and is now in the hands of justice.

Jayen. A curse on you for that!—In the hands of justice! Oh, you ignominious hydra, true, not even unto yourself! Did I not tell you, resort to innocent freaks which should discourage him only? Did I not command you to do him no harm, no bodily or moral injuries? Did I not bid you beware of that, lest I should play another part?—By heaven, you shall feel for this!—I have always looked on you with a friend's fondness and confidence, and you know it. But of th's be assured, I'll do it no longer.

Mohr. Well, well there needs but this retort—since you are my enemy, I must beware, and in heeding that, I defy and curse you. I know the cause of your threats—which are as paltry as the enmity you bear me. You are in my power and you dare not execute them, lest I should unmask the contrivances of the vain pretender to the love of Aurora Mayflower.

Jayen. Fie, be not too sure of that—you speak like what you are. You have deceived me, treacherously deceived me and you shall amend for it. By heaven! you'll regret this!—A few days hence may find you as wretched as destiny e'er can make you.

Mohr. You know then what you are going to do?

Jayen. Yes—let me fairly warn you. You will not see me yet I will dodge your every step; I shall be present at the supreme moment to interfere with you, and when you fancy yourself most secure—you will be the more certainly in my power.—Do you understand?

Mohr. [Indifferent] I believe I do.

Jayen. You had better be certain!

Mohr. I don't see why I should misunderstand you.

Jayen. Then why not say so? These feminine evasions, which sound very pretty in the world, will not do here. I am stern now, with a certain possiblity before my eyes—living, as it were, in the light of suspicion, and those who deal with me, must deal plainly and truly.

Mohr. But were you not my accomplice? You employed me, and on *you* rests the blame for it all—all.

Jayen. Yes, and I will bear it all. But, of this be assured, I will atone for it now and right the innocent. Aurora will know this all, [Going to door] myself shall disclose it to her, unburdened then—Ignatius Mohr, tremble! [Exit]

Mohr. [Alone] Should I know that Leona betrayed me, he would not leave this place—alive!—Tremble! ha, ha, ha! Ignatius Mohr tremble—one short hour will see me far from Indianapolis. Max Hartfeld in the hands of justice, precisely where I contrived to place him; not for the special accomodation of the artless Jayen Faul, but to remove the impediment to my success. It is not to accomplish *his* object that I labored for, but this, [Takes out check] yes this, ha, ha, ha! To night, Max Hartfeld will sleep in a criminal's cell, and there he cannot stop the payment of this check!

Leona. [Enters] Methought I heard you call!

Mohr. [Fondly conducts her to chair] Sit here Leona, 'tis likely you need repose! [Sits beside her]

Leona. Ah, how glad I am to see you thus peacefully and content at my side.

Mohr. Why should I not be while you are my adored, devoted and obedient wife!—Listen Leona, I have some good news for you!

Leona. Say that you will begin repentance now.

Mohr. Do you see this paper? [Producing check] 'Tis a check on the Bank of Delphi, payable to Aurora Mayflower within one week from date.

Leona. Well, what does that concern me? [Leona who has taken it eventually places it on table]

Mohr. Why don't you see! It is so easy for you to pretend to be this Aurora Mayflower. I will take you to Delphi immediately. Aurora nor you are personally known there, and you can easily perform your part of the deception. The check will be cashed without deduction to the amount of five thousand dollars.—I have kept this from you 'till now; the proper moment has arrived, and we must loose not a minute's time. You see, we will step into a handsome fortune, then off to some distant foreign country and all will be lovely.

Leona. And all will be ruin and dishonor, you had better say! But how came it into your possession?

Mohr. Mr. Hartfeld gave it to me, saying, he did not know what it was.

Leona. That check given you by Mr. Hartfeld—were I to gain the world by it, I could not thus impose on this poor man's ignorance!—No, husband, we would step directly into a trap of your own setting!

Mohr. Never fear that, I know what I'm about. Max Hartfeld, the only obstacle to be feared, rests quite sure in a safe berth.

Leona. Ah, never can I consent to wrong any one thus!

Mohr. How can you refuse to once more make a man of me, whose ruin you are bewailing? It will wrong no one; he is worth more than thrice that amount, and otherwise it will go to one who has no more right to it than you have

Leona. Do you remember, when, after the death of your victim, you swore and avowed to repent and begin a new life under a new name, if I would once more stand by you; how you induced me, by assurances, to leave Chicago secretly at midnight, to tramp this far distance? Believe me, though it had been a path of thorns I would have suffered it, only to save you—your life, and now you would repay me with such kindness and recompense; would have me thus stand by you, dishonorably still, and with one step more on the path of iniquity, finally plunge you into the abyss of an eternal purgatory.

Mohr. You must be brief. I'm not disposed to listen to sermons now.

Leona. Is that your avowed atonement, your contrition, your penitence?

Mohr. There is time yet for that!

Leona. Do not ask this of me—dismiss this base thought, 'twill never make us happy! I will do anything for you, but this I cannot. Cease this life of depravity, fulfill your promise, begin to reform—and with heaven's best blessing upon us, the former days of our prosperity will return. I will stand by you, work for you day and night; and when sickness shall call you to retire from the gay and busy scenes of this world, I will follow you into your gloomy retreat; listen with attention to your "tale of symptoms" and administer the balm of consolation to your fainting spirit. And lastly, when death shall burst asunder every earthly tie, I will shed an ocean of tears upon your grave, and lodge the dear remembrance of our mutual affections deep into my heart!

Mohr. On my knees I implore you, only this time—

Leona. Do not kneel to me—kneel to God, your God who reads every human heart, the mighty protector of the right and innocent! [Nervously] Heaven knows I will have naught to do with such a wicked scheme

Mohr. [Rises indignantly, and with contempt] Indeed! So you are really going to resist, against, what you are pleased to call a wicked scheme, are you! [Lowering voice] See here, Leona, the cup of my endurance has overflown; you ought to know by this time, that I am not to be disobeyed! Do you understand me?

Leona. [Stands silent R]

Mohr. [Kicking her] Do you hear me?

Leona. Yes!

Mohr. Very good. I'm glad that you have condescended to honor me by acknowledging that you *do* hear me. Now, do you intend to obey?

Leona. Oh please--please do not force me to take any part in this scheme, I feel that a terrible punishment will come to you and I, if we try to perpetrate such a fraud. You know that I would be but a counterfeit of the real Aurora—I am your wife and not a friend in the world save yourself.

Mohr. Oh, then you claim that I am your friend?

Leona. Yes! oh, yes!

Mohr. And you wish me to remain so?

Leona. I do, indeed I do! Why to think that you did not care for me, would break my heart!

Mohr. So, so! you don't want to make me hate you?

Leona. Hate me! You hate me! Oh, my dear husband, I could not think of such a thing. I would rather live in eternal tortue, than to have you hate me! Why do you speak of such a thing? It is cruel—cruel to admit, that such a thing is possible! [Sinks on knees, conceals face, resting head on chair]

Mohr. Oh, pshaw!—I'll risk her, I've seen women cry before.

Leona. Oh, heaven forgive him!

Mohr. [Seizing her roughly, throws her across to L] Get up and let us talk business! I want this matter settled right off.

Leona. Are you not yet satisfied? What would you have me do?—That which in all the trials of hardships and sufferings in this life with you, I have not yet even dreamt of,—imprecate the everlasting curses of heaven upon you! You have your wish; you cursed *me*, and that curse now curses you. I do not pray for you to die, but that you may live—live long and anloe, avoided by all that is human; hated by everyone, and in a life of lasting remorse —once imploring for compassion—be answered only by your own conscience.

Mohr. Oh, bosh! Stop your prating! You'll do it yet, I *know* you will. I am sure you will. [Shows revolver]

Leona. Never! heaven forbid it—never! [Seeing revolver] Yes, I will die first rather than live dishonored and disgraced.

Mohr. Ha, do you defy me, proud and boasting rebel?

Leona. Proud! Ha, ha, ha! well said—well said!—Yes, and

with defiance and boastingly too I confess, that I am too proud to submit to the baseness of a sway like yours!

Mohr. You forget whom and what you are.

Leona. Oh, no, not so fast! But who has made me what I am? You—and you know it. Weak I am as a child; but, strong in determination as adamant, against which your coarse threats recoil, but to their own destruction.

Mohr. Oh, adamant you *are*—and what am *I*, I should like to know?

Leona. Be what you may, I dare you to your worst.

Mohr. Ah, *you* do, do you?

Leona. Yes I, whose heart you have ground to powder beneath your iron heel, whose blood you have drained drop by drop, 'till existence becomes an active, poisonous curse. Yes, I can tell you what you are—for alas I know you well! A slimy, slow creeping animal, a reptile, a serpent that creeps to its prey slyly and meanly.

Mohr. A serpent am I—

Leona. A low, villainous wretch, eager for a crime that can be done in the dark, shrinking from a brave deed to be acted in open day; a villain who—thrusting an innocent heart into sin—sucks the lifeblood of its womanhood like a vampire!

Mohr. By heaven, to be thus braved by a woman! This pertinacity must be removed root and branch, though some blood be spilled in the operation! [Forces her down] You drive me to despair! Are you ready to obey?

Leona. Have pity on me! Heaven protect me!

Mohr. [Draws knife] Do you hear me? Yes, or no?

Leona. Your blessing first—your blessing—

Mohr. Yes, or no?

Enter Max, C D bareheaded, coat torn down back, coolly advances, takes knife from Ignatius, throws him off to R.

Max. *No!*—Dat's wat *I* toll you. Don you vas ashame! Move an unner shtep, un I make one hole in your big, black heart!

Mohr. Do you think that I fear you?

Max. No sir, I bin not afraid on you, wen you vas de devil, I bin not afraid on you. [Throws knife to his left so that he stands between it and Ignatius, then his coat] Come on! [Ignatius advances to Max who dodges him, Ignatius runs on and is about to take up knife when Max seizes him at back. Ignatius turns, backs Max across to R who then forces him back to L, throws him off and keeps Ignatius' false beard in his hand. Ignatius L with a large scar on his left cheek]

Leona. [In the meantime has run to C D as looking for help] Hold! for heaven's sake I pray you forbear!

Max How was dat? I pull de bottom von dat fellers head off!

Mohr. [Aside] I must win him now, or I am lost—[Aloud] Ha, ha, ha! why Max, you are indeed brave and fearless as the lion! I only did this to try your courage.

Max. Is dat so!—Well I dink you dry mine courage so many. I vas blenty mad I pooty near kill you after wile ago.—You vas black on your sheek! [Seeing scar]

Mohr. [Aside] Curses on him—indeed! probably from the little tussle we enjoyed a moment ago.

Leona. [Has come down to Ignatius] Ignatius—

Mohr. [Aside to her] Don't give tongue now, be off with you! [She retires up to table]

Max. Vor wat vor you do dat in your face? [Showing beard]

Mohr. Oh, only to look like a man—a natural one I cannot boast of.

Max. Is dat all! well I don't want em! [Throws beard front of table; takes up his torn coat, puts it on] You see dat coat? He vas ashame on me wen I gone on de shtreet.

Mohr. Oh, that's nothing, I'll give you another. Leona, go get my dark brown for this gentleman. [Exit Leona]

Max. Ye-e-s, I vas a shentlemans, ha, ha, ha!—When dat boliceman take me long he pull mine coat, awer I gone de unner way—[imitating the tearing] un he tear em; un wen I come up mit a shtreet dere vas a feller wat holler rags! rags! un wen he see me he say wat you do mit em regs? I gif you two cent!—I toll him dat vas not mine bustness, den he laugh me out like a dam geeses un gone away. Ye-e-s, shoor! Awer wen I have him here I pull his head out between his ears.

Re-enter Leona with coat, gives it to Max.

Leona. Here is the coat!

Max. Ah, you vas a good womans! [Patting her cheek] I like you! [Steals a kiss, then smiling, ogles Ignatius who eyes him] Wat's de matter on you? [Puts on coat which is tight fit]

Mohr. Oh, nothing—

Max. I dot I make you shelly.—Dat coat fit me ust so quick like skin on balony.—You know wat I toll you?

Mohr. Well!

Max. You vas a liar! you toll me everydings wat I eat down shtairs don't cost nottings, un dat vas not so: ven I vas done he toll me I must bay dat. Un den dere vas a grazy womans wat toll me I promise her I marry mineself, un dat vas not so, awer I don kno who she vas. Den I gone on de shtreet un dey run me after mine-self un toll de boliceman, I was a sheat, a willain un a shwindler —dat boliceman he toll me I must gone mit him, awer he not toll me dat vor de second time, he was glad wen he leave me alone. [Retires when Leona who was reading the check, anxiously waiting the opportunity to give it to Max]

Mohr. Fate must have made it a task to thwart me. When I thought him safest and most secure, he comes—despite my exertions—at the supreme moment to make my project almost an impossibility. But he shall have a hard road to travel now. [Sees Max who is examining the check] Damn the luck!

Max. (Comes down to Mohr) You sheat, you willain, you shwindler! you know wat at vas? (Showing check)

Mohr. (Goes to take it) Let me see—I—

Max. I dink you kno pooty well wat at was! Don't be in a hurry, I take care on em! (Folds and places it in his pocket)

Mohr. Perdition! everything seems leagued against me He shall not leave this place, he knows my secret and might noise it abroad. There is but this resort—his life or it will cost me mine—(Draws revolver, Leona sees this and screams. Max is about to exit but turns as Ignatius levels it and fires. Leona seizes his arm, throws it up, discharging the weapon in the air)

Leona. Harm him, cowardly as you would, and I'll betray you! (Clings to him)

Max. Hold on I fix em! (Exit in haste)

Mohr. Cling not to me! off, viper off! I must save myself—my life (Throws her off, rushes to C D) I must—hell he has escaped! *You* are the author of all this—take that—and that for your good service to me! (Runs down L. front where knife lies, takes it up, rushes furiously at Leona and stabs her in left side, she falls R C. Ignatius goes up to C D)

Leona. (Faltering) Ignatius, come hither husband—nay, do not shrink from your poor and sacrificed wife, now! Your hand; if I have wronged you, forgive me now, as I forgive you. Oh, Father of mercy! save and pity him!—I am dying, my heart is broken! Farewell! do not too soon forget me—repent—pray for me, I will pray for you—heaven bless you—farewell—fare—(Falls inanimate)

Mohr. (After short pause comes down to Leona, moves her with his foot) Dead!—You would betray me, would you!—There's *one* mouth shut up; dead people never tell tales. Ha, there's blood upon me—(Sees blood on right hand coat sleeve, exit in haste L I E)

Enter Oakdale C D.

Oakdale. (At door) I heard loud voices and the report of a shot, fired, methinks this is the room from which they issued. But, I see no one and all is quiet. Perhaps I may—(Advancing sees Leona, starts and stands terrified) Ha!—horrible—dead, and murdered too! Who could have done this! I'll know it--my honor is at stake, I'll bring the bloodhound, that could perpetrate this deed in my house, to light, though it should take me a diuturnity of years—hark!--I hear footsteps! I must not be seen, lest I be implicated. (Conceals)

Re-enter Ignatius who has changed coats, takes up beard, replaces it in his face.

Mohr. Adieu! cursed one, impediment to my success! You have your reward and may you be damned to endless flames, for you have ruined me, foiled me in everything. (Takes up hat)

The world is large and I must find another better and safer place now. (Exits C D but immediately returns)

Mohr. Ha! (Stands left of C D)

Re-enter Max, holding a gun straight out in front of himself. Ignatius gives him a severe blow on head and exits hastily.

Max. Now mine dear Shpitten Devil I vas ready. I—(The blow from Ignatius) Yeh!—Mine Gott in Himmel—I dot I vas in de unner world, I see de moon mit ten dousand shtars! I wonder who dat vas. I don't see me nobody! I vas not afraid on him wen he fight me like a shentlemans—awer pishtols, mine gootness, no sir! wen dat feller shoot me un hold dat pishtol ust dis way—puff'! un dat ball shoot me right away in de heart. Awer a feller like mine serwant wat vas no fatter as one herring, I shoot him mit a whole artilleries un I miss em wen I hit em! (Seeing Leona) Who's dat! (Places his gun against table, bends over her) Oh, mine Gott, dead! dat poor woman what I save mit her life, un wat she save my life—now she was dead! wen I vas outside, he kill dat poor woman!—Awer I shwear by mine honor, I find mine servant, I take him in dese hands un send him down in hell where his master it waiten on him!—Oh, when I vas mit her, I would be so glad so happy! She look so innocent, she was an angel now!—

Re-enter Ignatius with Bells Gap and others. Ignatius advances down L of stage.

Mohr. I accuse that man, Ignatius Mohr, with the murder of my wife! Secure him!

Max. (Rises) Wat! (Takes gun, raising it rushes at Ignatius. Officer averts the blow by seizing the gun. Tableau—Quick drop)

ACT IV. TABLEAU VI.

Interior of Court of Justice. Doors R I E and L behind spectators. Judge's bench R. Table and chairs R. Witness' stand R. Prisoners stand L I E. Max's gun and the broken blade on Judge's bench. Judge, Clerk, Ignatius, Shackles counsel for prosecution, twelve Jurymen arranged across back of stage. Spectators L. Officer, Jayen Faul who is one of the jury, disguised—all discovered.

Judge. The case Mr. Secretary to occupy the Court to-day is—

Clerk. (Reads aloud) That of alias Max Hartfeld, whose real name is supposed to be Ignatius Mohr, for the perpetration of the atrocious crime of murder, committed on the person of Leona Harfeld, the wife of the accuser.

Judge. Officer conduct the prisoner hither! (Exit Officer)

Mohr. (Aside) Ah, now I see my folly, 'twas imprudent of me to declare him to be Ignatius Mohr—but it's too late now, I cannot alter it. Anent that I must be on a careful gaurd 'till the proceedings are concluded; then, farewell to Indianapolis.

Max. (Without) All right! gone ahead, don you see I vas comen! (Enters L I E)

Officer. Make haste I say, the Court awaits you!

Max. (At entrance) Well, ust let em wait, dey wont run away. (Crosses to Clerk) I vas here!

Judge. Please take the stand

Max. (Rises on tip toes—to Judge) Don you see I shtand; I don see no shairs wat I sit down mit!—Dis place vas ust like mine cow stables, dere vas no benches un no shairs in dere, awer it vas full mit *bores* too

Clerk. Well, well, do you hear, take that stand! (Pointing to it)

Max. All right! why don you toll me dat right away? (Takes it to I E L) Where I take em? (Officer replaces it) Well, den you take em out. (Goes to railing front of jury, Officer conducts him to the stand, as he steps up he falls)

Judge. Why did you refuse a counsel for defense?

Max. No sir, I dont bounce dat fence! (Pointing to jury) Did I bounce dat fence wen I vas dere?

Judge. Understand me, I said, why did you refuse a counsel, a lawyer to—

Max. Ye-e-s! I dont need nobody wat toll you I did not make dat womans dead, I toll you dat mineself.

Clerk. Ignatius Mohr—

Max. Wat, Mohr—don I toll you my name vas not Mohr! you dink I f rgot mineself un say I vas somebody else? I vas nobody else, I vas mineself, Max Hartfeld!

Clerk. Or—as you choose to call yourself, Max—

Max. No sir, not Mex, Max—M-a-x—Max! I wonder wat shool you gone mit, don you kno better as dat?

Clerk. May it please you then *Max!* Do you swear by the Almighty and before this high Tribunal, that what you may say, shall be the truth, the whole truth and nothing but the truth?

Max. I shwear! You dink I toll you lies?

Cler. The affidavit made against you verifies: "that Leona, wife of Max Hartfeld, came to her death, by being fatally wounded with a bowie knife in the hands of Max Hartfeld, whose real name is Ignatius Mohr."

Shackles. The Coroner, when holding the inquest, found this broken blade, which is yet clotted with gore, imbedded in a gushing wound of the poor victim. Do you recognize or know this? (Holding broken blade up)

Max. No sir! how you dink I kno somedings wat I never see?

Shackles. The plaintiff will please take the stand!

Jayen. (Comes down from jury) May it please the Court! ere you proceed I would respectfully resign my duties as a juryman; I cannot now serve, therefore I beseech you to dismiss me.

Judge. What is the cause?

Jayen. A mission, which the near future may explain.

Judge. 'Tis granted!

Jayen. The broken blade—the missing part—adieu! (Bows to

Judge and bowing, turns to jury —Aside, going) '*Till we meet again!* (Exit)

Judge. In accordance to a statute which expressively stipulates, to convocate twelve men to act as a jury—we must now choose a substitute; the privilege of which I accord to the prisoner.

Mohr. (Rises) No, by heaven, I protest against such an illicit—

Max. (Runs from stand to Ignatius, vibrates his head perpendicularly) Wat's dat you say? uf you dont keep quiet I take you in mine hands un bulverize you!

Judge. Order there, sit down!

Max. Ye e-s, sit down! (To Ignatius)

Mohr. (To Max) You'll not be quite so lively after I've done with you. (Sits)

Max. Is dat so! Well I don't care!

Judge. Choose the substitute now!

Max. Ye-e-s, I will ! (Looks at spectators—suddenly) I dink I better gone dere mineself. (Sits on Jayen's place with the jury, busies himself with the next man at his side)

Judge. Oh, no, that won't do, come down immediately—do you hear— do you hear!

Max. (Comes down) Wat's de matter on you?

Judge. You have no business there, you—

Max. Don I vas a substishtood?

Judge. No, you are the prisoner, the defendant--anyone but yourself.

Max. Well, den I take dat man wat I vas shoor he toll you no lies. [Pointing him out, from the spectators]

Judge. The gentleman will please come forward !

Clerk. How do you swear? [Substitute raises his hand] Repeat as I dictate: " I do hereby solemnly swear, that with an honest and just judgment, to deliver truth on evidence given in Court."— Be seated ! [He sits on place vacated by Jayen]

Shackles. The plaintiff may now proceed.

Mohr. [Goes to stand R] Most honorable Judge! Gentlemen of the jury! Not many days ago, I came to this city, Indianapolis, accompanied by my wife, on a matter of business, and engaged a room in the Little Globe Hotel. I was within the city limits but a few hours, when I was grieved to learn, that the prisoner, with whom I am well acquainted, was imposing on my name and person.

Max. No sir, Mr. Shudge, I—

Judge. Keep quiet !

Mohr. After attending to my business matters, which occupied greater part of the day, I returned to the Little Globe Going up stairs to the room I occupied, which, by the way, is on the third floor, I heard deep groans of a person as in agony. Cautiously I slunk to the door, when I saw that man, quietly and unconcernedly, accoutering himself in that coat which he now wears and which is my own personal property—

Max. You *lie* dat! [Runs to Ignatius] Don you gif me dat coat—

Judge. Order there, take your place.

Max. Mr. Shudge—

Judge. Take your place and keep quiet 'till you are questioned!

Max. Well, I dont care! [Slowly returns to stand] Dat feller lie ust so fast as one horse wat run—I gif ten cents when I kno what shurch he belong mit.

Judge. Proceed.

Mohr. I was about to enter the room when another groan drew my attention to the floor, and—oh horror—what did I behold! My poor wife weltering in her own blood—just then, she faintly lifted her head and with a staring look at the culprit, she exclaimed: "you here—that knife in your hand—then you are my murderer"—

Max. You black villain— (throws officer's hat at Ignatius.) Dat vas not so—

Judge. I will inflict a fine of five dollars on you for disorderly conduct in Court.

Max. Wat's dat?

Judge. Five dollars fine for dis-or-der-ly conduct.

Max Allright! I give you five times five dollars fine — awer wat's de use he toll you dem big lies? I wonder he don't shoke on em!

Shackles. Hold your tongue! (Threatening)

Max. He got no handle on wat I hold em mit.

Shackles. We don't want to hear your opinions now.

Max. Well, den better you gone outside.

Shackles. (To Ignatius.) Go on.

Mohr. After uttering the word, " murderer," her voice faltered, a deep sigh—and my poor wife was no more. Her spirit is in a brighter home now and from that abode of eternal bliss, she watches over me with incessant vigilance.

Shackles. Was the prisoner cognizant of your presence?

Mohr. No!— But I saw him I saw her stately form drenched with it's own sacred blood; I saw the broken knife in his hand, reeking with—

Max. Dam lies! (Going to Ignatius) Awer now it vas time you keep quiet—(Threatening)

Judge. (Rising) Order, order—

Max. (Runs down to Judge) Mr. Shudge—

Judge. Order I say—

Max. I only toll you, dat—

Judge. Nothing, I'll hear nothing!

Max. (Runs to jury and gesticulates)

Judge. Order—do you hear—return to the stand immediately. Officer, do your duty. (Officer goes to Max who then returns to stand. Officer gets his hat and returns)

Judge. (Seriously) If you venture to leave that stand again, I will have you shackled and impose another and heavier fine on you, understand?

Max. All right Shudge—awer wat's de use you make so many noise?

Judge. (Sits again—to Ignatius) Continue.

Mohr. Alarmed and bewildered, I hastened to summon an Officer, which culminated in the capture and arrest of the felon. But what should have prompted him to commit this diabolical crime, I am at a loss to conjecture. This I swear by the Almighty Judge, to be the truthful statement relative to the event. (Leaving stand) Shackles. Stay—did you not say that he imposed on your name? What know you of his real name?

Mohr. He claims to be Max Hartfeld. But that is a name, unsullied, which I have the honor to bear. I have dealt with him ere now, his real, true name is Ignatius Mohr and—

Max. (Runs to C taking stand with him) Mr. Shudge—

Judge. (Provoked, throws a book at Max, not noticing removal of the stand. Max dodges as book passes over his head) Keep quiet! (Max in stand C looks at book on floor L)

Max. Five dollars fine for dis-or-der-ly corndooctor!

Judge. (Vexed) Yes, ten dollars fine for leaving the stand.

Max. (Looks at Judge, then where the stand was, then at stand and then stares at Judge who rises and gazes at Max and the stand—short pause)

Judge. You have moved the stand from it's proper place.

Max. You only find et out now?

Judge. Take it back immediately.

Max. All right! (Returning with stand) Dat's de time wat you, fool me, he! Ten dollars fine when I leave dat shtand, ha, ha, ha' you better look out, I vas not so shtoophead as you look.

Judge. Order now!

Mohr. He arrived in town here about half an hour before myself. No sooner did he learn of my presence, than he roamed about, pretending to be myself, Max Hartfeld, though I positively assert and declare here, that he is Ignatius Mohr from the city of Chicago. The proof of what I say is in his possession; an overdue promisary note. So much so true. (Leaves stand)

Max. So much dam lies!

Judge. Order—keep your place a moment, please! — Officer search him.

Max. No sir, I search me mineself. (Finds the note, which Ignatius knew was in the coat) Mr. Shudge, dat feller he toll you after wile ago I shteal dat coat, un dat vas not so. Mine unner coat he tear me, un dat feller he say he be mine servant wat cost nottings un toll me his name vas Shpitten Devil. Well, he gif me dat coat, un he kno pooty well dis papers vas in.

Judge. Officer, bring that paper to me.

Max. (Runs to Judge) Here Shudge! (Gives it)

Judge. Hm! true—"Chicago, September the third" and signed

"Ignatius Mohr."—But a-a-so by this you mean to prove his real name, do you?

Mohr. Precisely I do.

Judge. Exactly! I see And but five minutes ago you alleged to have seen him inappropriating that very coat to his own use, and decidedly asserted it to be your *own personal property.* Agreed. There is then this corollary; the coat belonging to you, this note, undersigned Ignatius Mohr, being found in this same coat—belongs to you also.

Shackles Mr. Judge, I en neatly protest against your procedure, which is conterminal to privileges that are—

Judge. Order!

Shackles. 1 am in order.

Judge. You are not—a word and I will grant an injunction on you for contempt of Court. That man has no counsel for defence, and if he is seemingly imposed upon, it becomes my bonden duty as *Judge,* to protect and give him justice. (Shackles sits. Judge abruptly to Ignatius) That will do, you may retire. (Ignatius comes down, when Max interposes him)

Max. Hold on, I toll you somedings.

Mohr. (Roughly] Well !

Max. You liar shbalben! you better look out wen you ketch me outside—I vas in a *free* country now, un I bin *not* afraid on a dirty blackguard like you! (Flourishing his fist under Ignatius' nose)

Mohr. (With contempt) Ha, ha, ha! (Takes his seat)

Max. (Imitating) Ha, ha, ha!—Wat's de use you laugh me out? When dese dogs (His clenched hands) pick you up un shake you one little bit un drow you out—den you find nottings wat you laughen mit - 1 vas no wonder wen I do dat right away. (Rushing at Ignatius)

Judge. Order dow, that won't do here, take your place in the stand.

Max. (Recollecting) Well dats so, ha, ha, ha! I forgot all about em. (Goes to stand)

Judge. The next to take the stand Mr. Secretary, is—

Clerk. " Bells Gap an Officer." [Reading]

Judge. Take the stand.

Clerk. [Rises] Do you swear by the Almighty and before this high Tribunal assembled; That what you may say, shall be the truth, the whole truth and nothing but the truth?

Officer. I swear.

Judge. What know you in regard to this case?

Shackles. You arrested the prisoner, did you not?

Officer. Yes sir, I did

Shackles. You will state particularly all you know.

Officer. On the morning of that fatal day, I was walking the street on patrol duty, I was intercepted by that man, the plaintiff. By a little revelation he invariably established to me, at once, his veracity and honor. '' I am a stranger here," he continued, "and am teazed to death by a certain individual, a scoundrel, who is imposing on my name and honor." Describing the villain, he requested me to apprehend him. At the same time he also told me, that his own name was Max Hartfeld, from Delphi, in corroboration of which he handed me a letter of recommendation and credit.

Max. Ye-e-s, well dat vas mine; he vas mine servant un I give him dat letters.

Judge. [Calmly] Order please—[To Officer] go on.

Officer. Subsequently, I encountered this impostor amidst a conflux of people, who pursued and vituperated him for various offences. Despite my efforts to secure him then, he escaped me.

Max. Ye-e-s, uf you dont gone away at time, I scrape you pooty well, ha, ha, ha!—

Judge. Order there, you criminate yourself!

Officer. On that very day, scarcely five hours later, I chanced to pass by the Little Globe Hotel, when the plaintiff hastily approached and excitedly bade me follow him; that his wife was brutally murdered, and, that the perpetrator was yet in the house. —When we entered the room, the prisoner was bending over the body of his victim—seeing his jeopardy, in a fit of rage, he seized a gun and would have killed his accuser, but for my opportune interference.

Shackles. [Showing gun] Is this your gun?

Max. Ye-e-s, dats my gun.

Shackles. How do you account for having that gun at a place and time, which invariably evinces the evidence of your guilt?

Max. Well, you see dat gun vas mine, I buy me dat gun—I take dat gun *mit* me—I vas in dat room—un you vas a shackass uf you dink at gun vas not dere too.

Shackles. [To Officer] Have you anything more to say?

Officer. No sir! 'Tis easy to surmise what followed. [Leaves stand]

Shackles. The arrest, certainly!—There are no other witnesses—

Clerk. Convicting—none.

Judge. Now Max—

Max. *Max*, wen you blease!

Judge. What have you to say in vindication of yourself?

Max. Windy—wat? You dink I vas a blowbag? No sir, I toll you de druth!

Judge. I don't dispute that. But, what have you to say in justification against censure—

Max. Senses! yes shoor, I got blenty senses. [Tapping his forehead with his fist]

Judge. Keep quiet now and wait.

Max. All right, why don you say so!

Judge. Understand me, it is your turn to speak now; I mean you to explain everything concerning the charges against you; if you *are* the murderer or *not*, and prove your innocence.

Max. I know—shoor—I know wat you mean allatime—awerrr

wats de use you say I vas windy? I dont blo so many!—Don I toll you I dont make dat womans dead?

Judge. Will you swear it?

Max. Yes sir—by da—hello Pete what you maken here? [Runs to juror on the opposite]

Judge. Order there, take your place.

Max. [Returns having mistaken the man] I dot you vas somebody else wat I kno.

Judge. Never mind that now. Go on, the Court is ready to listen to you.

Max. Was it well I like dat — Mr. Shudge! Shentlemens who vas on a Shury!--Dat feller [Pointing to Ignatius] he vas mine servant, now dont forgot et! he make me so many trubles un toll blenty lies—You vas a liar, a dief, a villain, a shwindler, a rascal, a shwindler, a scoundrel—

Shackles. We don't want to know what he is, we desire to learn what *you* are.

Max. Well, den you better find et out.—Mr. Sbudge—[Shackles murmurs] Order! [To Shackles]—I gone in mine servant's room, un when I vas outside, I hear somebody wat tell somebody else, "yes oder no!" den I hear nobody wat say noddings, den I hear somebody ·av an un er time, "yes oder no!"—den I comes in, un you kno wat I see? dat nkly rascal he have dat woman on a floor un got one big knife wat he say, "yes oder no!" [Spirited] I shnatch me dat knife, I take dat dog un drow him away un say— No!—Don I say dat, don I say dat? [To Ignatius]

Mohr. *The man's mad—heed him not*—let him prove it—*he knows not what he says!*

Max. You find et out after while.—Den he toll me, he vas only sho en—I dink it vas a pooty shentle shoken, dat poor womans she gry ust like a shild, un her sheeks run down mit tears, yes —After while I find mine sheck mit five dousand dollars un den I gone out, when he see dat, he was mad un he shoot me, awer dat good womans she knock dat pishtol away. When he fight me dis way [Showing fists] I was a man—awer pishtols, no sir! I gone right away down on de shtreet un gone in dat shtore wat have dree balls out on a shtring un I buy me dat gun. When I come back mit at room, I say. "now I vas not afraid on you!"—awer I see nobody— wen somebody hit me on de head, dis way—[Gives Officer, who is next the stand a blow on the head] ye e·s, he pooty near knock me sensib'e! I dot I get de shpasms—shoor, dats wat for I toll you.— Den I find me dat good womans wat I save mit my life—she was dead! she was dead—when I was outside un buy me dat gun, he have an unner shance, un like a dog he kill dat poor woman— [With increasing exci ement] I was mad, I shwear when I find mine servant I have revenge! he was here now—I take him mit his neck un I kill—[Greatly excited rushes at Ignatius, seizes and pulls him from his seat throwing him across to L C, then rushing forward at him again, he is intercepted by the Officer.—The Court has risen—picture]

Judge. Officer, conduct him to the stand and guard the entrance.

Mohr. [Aside] I defy him, he cannot prove one solitary word of it. [Retires]

Max Wen I catch em dat time I squeeze em like dough.

Judge. Proceed now.

Max. Well, I vas in dat room ust pout two minutes, wen mine servant, dat perjured willain, comes in mit a boliceman un he tell em, rest me I kill his wife. Now Mr. Shudge, dats *so*, de *whole* so, un nodding *but* so. I could not tell a lie, un uf you heng me right away, I would not tell *one* lie. When I vas a little boy, my poor, dear Mutter she toll me: "Max," she say, "never tell a lie—never tell a lie."—She vas *dead* now, awer I dont forgot et; when I bin fifty years old, I will *never* forgot what my poor, dead Mutter toll me so many times!

Shackles. How often, did you say, you struck your adversary?

Max. I dont shtruck em at all. I only hit em two times; de first time wat I hit em, I miss em, un de secon time, I hit em on de same blace.

Judge. Then you did not strike him at all?

Max. Ye-e-s, sir, I-I-well dats so.

Shackles. Have you no witness to testify in your behalf?

Max. Dere was nobody else dere, you know it pooty well.

Mohr. Certainly not, how *could* he have?

Enter Oakdale R.

Oakdale. I will answer that! and if 'tis somebody that cannot fully establish his innocence, he can at least—turn over a new leaf!

Mohr. What, you? Oakdale—impossible!

Oakdale Impossible! Then be assured that this is the first possible impossibility.

Mohr. Why, you did not even witness the arrest, see:

Judge. Mr. Secretary, swear him. (Oakdale goes to stand)

Shackles. Mr. Judge, I most emphatically protest—

Max. Wat's dat—(goes to run from stand but officer prevents him)

Shackles. Against that man taking the stand under oath—

Max. Mr. Judge—

Judge. Order—

Shackles. Besides, he would be an in—

Judge. ⎱ Order— (rises) order— (still to shackles.)

Max. ⎰ Keep quiet—Mr. Shudge—

Shackles. He would be an indirect—

Judge. Order—

Max. Mr. Shudge I toll you somedings—

Shackles. (Turning to Max) You are guilty—

Judge. Order, I command—

Max. Mr. Shudge—

Shackles   (Still to Max) You have plainly shown (Judge em
barrassed.)

Max. Order, Mr. Shudge—

Shackles. (Receiving no attention, turns to Jury) Circumstan--
tial evidence, clearly, positively and most infalibly points to his
guilt; besides, he made the self convicting statement that no living
soul else *did* witness the deed.

Max. Mr. Shudge, Shtop dat gass off (pointing to Shackles)

Judge. Mr. Shackles will be pleased to seat himself. Mr.
Dawsillet you may speak.

Oakdale. I am the proprietor of the " Little Globe Hotel" I was
busily engaged when I heard loud voices, and a few minutes later, a
shot fired. As soon as I could leave my post of duty, I proceeded up
stairs at once; on entering the room, occupied by the plaintiff
and his wife, I saw noboby and all was quiet. Foreboding something serious—as I never liked the looks of that man, his suspective
demeanor, his doubtful integrity, and questionable veracity—

Shackles. Stop.

Max. Keep quiet, you got no bustness—

Shackles. You are assuming a phase accusative—

Judge. Order.

Max. Yes, sit down, it was a good ding I don't got you now
oder—(leaning on railing it breaks, falls to the floor) Mr. Court,
ust wait one little bit, I fix em. (Bends over stand but cannot
reach it, leaning on the stand, his weight breaks the front out,
which falls into an inclined position. Max falling also, slides
down the plane on his belly—I mean abdomen) Dat shtand break
me down un shlide me out. (Returns perplexed, as though nothing
had happened, cooly facing audience and leaning on that side.)

Judge. Don't be excited, take it cool, and—

Max. Shoor. Dat's wat I say.

Judge, You will break up the Court if you continue in this
manner.

Max. Well you kno dat's my fashion.

Judge. (To Oakdale.) Proceed.

Oakdale. Not yet satisfied, I advanced into the room and there
I found the lifeless body of the alleged Mrs. Hartfeld. A moment
later, I heard footsteps, fearing to be discovered, alone, with the
body, I concealed myself to avoid an impeachment on my part,
which, would certainly h ve been the inevitable consequence.

Shackles. Permit me to ask you one question—

Max. You big wing shnakefeeder rattleshnake—(placing his
hand on Shackle's head, forces him down) sit down !

Shackles. (To Oakdale.) That will do, you may sit down.

Oakdale. When I am ready, if you please !—From my hiding
place I saw this man, the prosecutor, entering from the adjoining
room, in great haste and iritation, his cautious lcok betraying an
intricate anxiety which generally accrues to an atrocious crime.
He stooped to the floorbut what he did then, I could not see.

When he left the room, I heard a shriek, a man stood at the door, apparently stunned—

Max. Dat vas me, Mr. Shudge, don I toll you dat? Den it was dat cow what hit me on de head—ooh—I will gratch your eyes out!

Shackles. You will like to do more than that, after we have done with you. Do you endeavor with your assumed indifference and droll humor, at so grave a trial as this, to influence the Jury and obtain a verdict in your favor?

Max. Wat's de use I gry? I comes free,. I don't make dat womens dead, un an udder ding : when I vas mit sensible peoples, (pointing off stage) I was sensible, too ; awer when I was mit lunadics all round (pointing about at Shackles and Ignatius) den I was blendy luny too, un you never find et out

Judge. Mr. Dawsillet, proceed.

Oakdale. In a moment that man advanced, only to behold the same dire spectacle that I did. Startled with amazement, he knelt beside the corse and audibly swore to meet his servant and avenge the death of that "poor woman,"—at this juncture he was surprised by an officer, and the husband of the victim, who charged him with the murder.

Shackles. Why did you absent yourself from the scene of trial until now, to thus expugn the Court and attempt to sway the Jury?

Max. (pointing off) Se uf you don't gone out now, I git somebody wat will gone out !

Oakdale. I can answer that; because I could not leave my business until now; besides, it pleases me extremely, that to your disappointment and disgust, I just came in time to succeed in an attempt, as yau say, to sway the Jury as it were : because I have told facts, downrtght plain facts, against which, your prolate dexterity stands abashed.

Shackles. After hearing the shot fired, how soon did you arrive at the bloody scene ?

Oakdale. About ten minutes.

Shackles, You intimate that the plaintiff committed the murder himself ?

Oakdale. I did not say so. Inasmuch, I did not see that.

Shackles. When you entered the room, you saw the prisoner bending over the body ?

Oakdale. (Pointedly) No sir,—I said that I saw nobody and all was quiet.

Schackles. Oh, you saw nobody—I see !—Have you anything more to say ?

Oakdale. No sir, I have spoken.

Shackles. That will do, then,—Gentlemen of the Jury ! From the testimony given, you will see, that the prisoner was found alone with the murdered body ; he had a gun or musket with him, which he claims to be his own and with which, on seeing the plaintiff, he also attempted to assault him. I may tell you, too, that the prisoner entertained an ill feeling toward the plaintiff and his victim, especially the wife of the plaintiff. The concoction given by the witness, who so bluntly turned up in favor of him, has very little weight in this case : he says he found *no one* with the body, albeit the fact to the contrary, that the prisoner was arrested beside the body. Indeed, I question whether he knew anything about the tragedy, 'till after the arrest. Now gentlemen, the prisoner did not plausibly explain how he came to be in that room—alone with the body—and why he bought this gun but five or ten minutes before the blooby deed, as he, himself, testified ; this alone would warrant a verdict against him. Taking all this into consideration, why then gentlemen, what shall your verdict be ?

Judge. Gentlemen of the Jury ! You have heard the evidence for the prosecution—evidence full of discrepencies and statements of the most conflictive, improbable and contradictory kind. The plaintiff, at the beginning of his statement, very consciously claimed that the prisoner wears a coat, surreptitiously obtained from his, the plaintiff's room, and subsequently he contradicted his assertion, by referring to a note in said coat and then saying he did not mean to express that the prisoner had stolen the coat. Now gentlemen, this is a fact that must be taken into consideration. —On the other side, you have heard the evidence of the prisoner ; It was a congenial statement spontaneously uttered with a firmness and consistency that evinces the utmost truth. Besides, the plausible testimony of Mr. Dawsillet, fully concurs with and corob-orates what the prisoner has said. The question then is ; Did the prisoner inflict the fatal wounds ? In this case you must say, guilty; if, on the other hand, you believe what the prisoner and his witness have told you, then you must say, *not guilty.* Therefore, gentlemen, in the absence of all positive proof—for nothing that we have heard here, has verified it—you will retire. and may providence enlighten and direct your minds. to find a just and proper verdict. (Sits, Jury rises and exits, door R I E) Officer, lead the prisoner back to his cell. (As the last Juryman is about to exit, Max detains him, whispers and then)—

Max. Don you believe it. [Turns, sees Aurora who has entered] Aurora!

Aurora· Oh, Max! [They embrace]

Mohr. [Aside] So that is Miss Aurora—I should like to command her myself !

Aurora. They told me you would not be called for the hearing 'till noon and but now, perchance, I learned that you had already been tried and found guilty. Tell me it is not true?

Max. Drue! No, don you believe it, I dink it vas all lies.— Awer—dat feller—ooh—[Breaks embrace, towards Ignatius but immediately returns] he say he make me square mit me, dey heng me anyhow; on I vas ust so innocent like a shild !—Aurora, come an see me, wen I'm hanged !

Aurora. Do not despair now and speak thus. You are innocent, I *know* you are. Stand firm—this base, villainous, perjured
imposter will yet be foiled and your innocence in exulataion triumph.

Max. Well dat so! I was —ooh I was grazy. Aurora, you
was a good girl, now I bin so happiness like after wile ago,

Officer. (Who has received the verdict, gives it to the Judge.)
The verdict!

Judge. (Surprised) What—so soon!

Aurora. Quick, Mr. Judge, what says the Jury?

Judge. (Looks at it, short pause and regrettingly, replies)
guilty! (Aurora screams and staggers; Max supports her)

Max· Aurora, " *shtand firm, dis base willain, impostor, will yet
be foiled and your innocence in exultation triumph.*" You see, I
don't forgot wat you toll me. (Ignatius has come to L, front.)

Judge. Is it possible, that in the face of such convincing
evidence, the Jury could say, guilty !—the prisoner will take leave
now and retire.

Mohr. Mr. Judge, I thank you! May I honorably take leave
now?

Judge. Honorably! (?)— (Aside) Indeed very.—Yes!

Mohr. (Hypocritically smiling, to Max) Adieu! Mr. Mohr,
I will see you later.—Now farewell to Indianapolis—[is about to
exit when enters Jayen Faul—Shackles has risen, the Judge is
also preparing to leave.]

Jayen. [Still disguised] Not so fast, Mohr, I have another
account for you to balance—stop, I command you! [As he passes
the officer—to whom—] Be on the guard.

Mohr. Who is it that commands—

Jayen. Mr. Judge, I accuse that man, Ignatius Mohr, with the
murder of his wife. Max Hartfeld is innocent,

Max. See dat, don I toll you.

Mohr. What—a *stranger* accuse *me* with the murder of my wife ?
Folly! Prove it—prove it, that is all.

Jayen. Yes prove it. The cowardly craven who secretly kills
in the *dark*, may well cry for proofs of its base deeds, and then
prate of and feign innocence, but despite that, I have caged the
birdie and will cut its wings now !

Max. Un den I catch em and un pull his fedders out!

Jayen. You ask for proofs, do you? You shall have them.
Disprove you then that this coat [which Ignatiusconcealed in the
third act—light colored] stained with blood, was not worn by you
on the day of and previous to the murder; disprove you then, that
this broken knife, stained with blood and your name engraved on it,
prove that it is *not* yours. [Produces the knife from coat, takes
the broken part from Judge's bench, holds them together.] Mr.
Judge, I believed the prisoner was innocent It was I who resigned
from the Jury and hastened straightforward from here to the
rooms of the inhuman monster, to search for evidence of his guilt ;

it was I who found his coat there, concealed in the ventilator flue and in *it*, the missing part of the broken knife; It is I who now boldly stands here and dares assert and suppliment my first charge with another—that of corrupt solicitation, that by this putrid mass of corruption, the *Jury* was *bribed*!

Judge and Aurora. Bribed!

Judge. By heaven, I suspected this!

Jayen. Yes, bribed to render a verdict against the prisoner—ha! [Sees Jurymen returning from R I E door, runs forces them back.] Back I say, all—every one of you! [Locks door and withdraws the key] Now, gentlemen of the Jury, comfort yourselves in there, 'till the law rewards you for your honest treachery!

Max. Ha, ha, ha! Adieu, Mr. Mohr, *I will see you later.* [Imitating Ignatius.]

Mohr. Is it not likely that the prisoner himself, placed the broken knife in one of my coats, concealed it there to avoid suspicion and subsequently pretend to *find* the coat, and thus throw the guilt on me? This man comes here maliciously inclined, despising me for one thing or another, to influence and deceive, or mislead you? I defy him, whoever he may be! who are you?

Jayen. [Throws off disguise] Jayen Faul!-[all start]-Ah, shrink not, look not amazed! do you know me now—your old friend, but now your enemy! It is *my* turn now and we will settle our differences in my own way. Remember Ignatius—*I am playing another part!* What say you now?

Mohr. What *should* I say! Why should I shrink from, look amazed or fear you? I know you not and still *less* do *you* know, who and what *I* am.

Jayen. But, unfortuately for you, I only know too well, who and what you are : A base, villainous, degraded and treacherous sneak ; a meanly and *yet* smoothly polished hypocrite, the murderer of your wife.

Mohr. What! I a murderer!—A husband murder his wife! Impossible. She was always to me, a loyal companion in sorrow and joy; a devoted wife—I loved her with all a husband's fondness and affection, and was ever ready to sacrifice my heart's blood for her, drop by drop. Is it likely then, that I could in cold blood, murder, or even in the least, harm a beloved and faithful wife?

Jayen. Reprobate hypocrite! (Half aside)

Max. *Dat man's mad, hit em not, he kno not wat he say!*

Jayen. Fie! despite your relished eloquence, your pretended sorrow, your apparent bewailment and vain hypocrisy—it is likely and *possible* too. Do not affect wonder, when I tell you, that your wife, herself confided to me your infidelity and cruelty towards her, and that to escape justice and capital punishment, you fled secretly from Chicago at midnight and came here with an assumed name—

Mohr. Prove it, ha, ha, ha! she is *dead* now, prove it if you can.

Jayen. A fugitive from justice there, you are a refugee in justice here, under whose infallible scrutiny you will assuredly receive a murderer's reward.

Mohr. *Always give the devil his just dues,* so let him whose deeds merit such a reward, receive it—not I !—Have I been committed, tried and convicted ?—You *have* the answer. See! ha, ha, ha—

Enter George Cleveland, the detective.

Cleveland. Which of you is Ignatius Mohr?

Mohr. Hell and damnation, I'm tracked !—(Suddenly) This man here, a convict! (Pointing to Max)

Max. Don you believe it! I ves Max Hartfeld, von Delphi.

Cleveland. (Surveys Max) That man?—No! immpossible.

Max. Dat's wat I say! (To Ignatius and the others) See dat, see dat, see dat! Dat man toll you I vas nobody else, I was mineself Max Hartfeld—he, he, he! How *you* kno dat, who vas you?

Jayen. This man, I swear it, is Ignatius Mohr, a criminal fugitive from Chicago.

Cleveland. (Starts suddenly) What—no, he is not the Ignatius Mohr that I am searching for, he does not answer the description.

Mohr. (With mock contempt) Ha, ha, ha! (To Jayen) Where are you now? You would swear it, would you? Well that pleases me! Ha, ha, ha! (Aside) He is so near to me and yet so far—I defy them all.

Cleveland. Mr. Judge—I presume?—

Judge. I am.

Cleveland. My interruption here demands an explanation.— Two weeks ago, a young girl was most savagely murdered in Chicago, by an inhuman wretch, who then succeeded in the attempt to escape, unknown. Circumstances, subsequently led to the discovery of the perpetrator, a notorious character, one Ignatius Mohr, who in the meantime had suddenly disappeared. Diligent search was made, but no trace of him could be found. Yesterday, the Chief of the Secret Service at Chicago, was apprised of the arrest here, of a man supposed to be Ignatius Mohr. I have a warrant for his arrest, and here is a description of him: " He is a man of average stature, strong, but not stout, hair—black, and on the left side of his face, which is fair and beardless, he has an unmistakable brand, a broad mark or scar, which he received in a deadly combat."—

Mohr. But you see, there is no such identical person amongst us, so if you desire to continue the search elsewhere, certainly, *we will detain you no longer.*

Cleveland. Indeed! sarcastic savant! I will trouble you no longer—adieu! (Goes to entrance—Aside) I strongly suspect the insolent deportment of that man! (At entrance) Were it not for that agreeable beard of yours, I should dare say, you are the very man.

Mohr. (L C) Why you do not mean to say or suspect—

Max. Hold on!—Dat beard—dat mark mit his face--I dink me on somedings, I show you! (Seizes Ignatius, they contest)

Mohr. Ah, you would--

Max. Villain, I got you now! [Pulls false beard from Ignatius' face and points triumphantly at the scar] See!

Mohr. Betrayed—now could I drink hot blood ! By hell you shall fall with me! [Levels revolver at Max]

Max. Don you—[Detective in turn draws on Ignatius]

Cleveland. Hold !

Max. [Runs, jumps on chair then on table, takes gun from Judge's stand and also levels it at Ignatius] Now shoot uf you blease! [Picture--Max on table, Detective R, Ignatius L—general excitement aud great surprise]

Mohr. Damn the luck, I'm undone now, betrayed despite myself, ruined, foiled in everything!

Max. [Has come down] Well, mine dear Shpitten Devil, how you feel now? *Maybe you vas only shoken, he!*

Cleveland. Mr. Mohr, in the name of the law, I arrest you, you are my prisoner.

Mohr. By what authority—who are you?

Cleveland. George Cleveland, the detective! Will you submit?

Mohr. With my life only!

Cleveland. It is useless for you to resist any longer.

Mohr. Back!—Damn it I'll cheat them yet! [Shoots himself, reels, Shackles goes to support him] Off with you, do not touch me—[Throws him off--hysterically, with force exerted] Ha, ha--ha--ha! Now I am your's *take* my body, and [Defiantly] if you would have my soul, pursue it down to hell--yes you, *all* of you—and there we shall meet—ha! [Falls with a horrible groan—he is taken off by Officer and Shackles]

Max. *Always gif de devil his dues*—well, I dink when *he* comes dere, de devil will gif em pooty many dues. Dat feller he talk so terrible—ooh—mine skin was ust like a geeses,—Well Shayen, you vas mine rival—

Jayen. Yes, and to gain the favors and love bestowed on you—for myself, I have caused you much grief and sorrow. But, now to make my atonement complete, I joyfully resign *all* my claims to the affections of Miss Aurora.

Max. Aurora, you hear dat? Shayen you vas a good feller, dat sheck wat I have for Aurora—[Brings it from pants pocket] mine rascal servant *he* have dat sheck, un he toll me I *loose* me dat sheck un he never find at check—well, I gif you dat sheck, dat vas your's now.

Jayen. You are very generous, and--

Max. Never mind wat I was—you save me mit my life, un I gif you dat sheck un I make you happy.—Awer you see, mine diabollicallical servant he was catch em in his *own* drap, un I vas free!

Aurora. Vice received it's recompense and virtue it's reward.

Max. Now Aurora you vas mine, now we gone in Delphi, un den we gone married !—[Tableau—Curtain]

—THE END.—

PERPLEXITIES.

CHARACTERS.

Max Hartfeld.—a German "von Delphi."
Jayen Faul.—Professor of Music.
Ignatius Mohr.—a "Chevalier d'industry" from Chicago.
Oakdale Dawsillet.—Proprietor of the " Little Globe."
Bells Gap.—an Officer.
Doctor Phaeton.—of the Lunatic Asylum,
Ninny Adam.—whose name indicates his character.
Min Cutts.—who fancies he is a King.
Lank.—who imagines he is of Glass.
Caracelli.—an Image Vender.
Judge Primrose.—
Mr. Vandim.—Clerk of Court.
Shackles.—Counsel for Prosecution.
George Cleveland.—a Detective in the Secret Service of Chicago.
Aurora Elena Mayflower.—in the Female College.
Leona Mohr.—Wife of Ignatius.
Madame DeRuyter.—Proprietress of the Female College.

Twelve Jurymen, Spectators, &c.

☞ The Scene is laid in Indianapolis, Indiana.